T5-DHD-063

THE
DEVILISH
MARQUIS

Karla Hocker

WARNER BOOKS

A Warner Communications Company

Warner Books, Inc.
666 Fifth Avenue
New York, N.Y. 10103

 A Warner Communications Company

Printed in the United States of America

First Printing: September, 1989

10 9 8 7 6 5 4 3 2 1

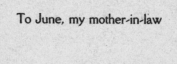

To June, my mother-in-law

Chapter One

When the solicitor stopped speaking, Nell heard only the wild beat of her own heart. All sounds from outside Miss Mofty's Select Academy for Young Ladies in Bath were muted by a blanket of snow. The corridors and stairways of the large house lay steeped in silence, for Miss Mofty's noisy, highborn pupils had not yet returned from their Christmas holidays.

The most junior of Miss Mofty's school mistresses huddled in a worn armchair in the tiny sitting room designated for the staff's use. Looking like a child herself, she raised her face to the gray-haired gentleman who had come down from London especially to see her. The smile on his lined countenance was fatherly as he stood facing her, warming his coattails in the meager comfort of the stove.

Hardly daring to believe in her good fortune, in the possibility of fulfilling her most ardent desire, Nell asked, "Could you—would you, please, repeat what you just said, Mr. Forsythe?"

"Yes, of course, Miss Hetherington." The solicitor met

Nell's clear gray eyes with a twinkle in his own. "Considering that Lady Augusta hid herself away in Cornwall and refused to enter into correspondence with her relations and friends these past fifteen years, I am not surprised that you find the news rather startling."

"I never once met my godmother. She died two months ago, you said? And left me her London house?"

"I would have notified you sooner, but it took me all of six weeks to locate you. And then the snow storm—"

"Mr. Forsythe," Nell interrupted. "That you found me at all is a miracle in itself. That Lady Augusta Fawnhope remembered me in her will is, well, it's quite fantastic. A house in London!"

"To be precise, it is only half of a house. The north half of Fane House, as it was known years ago. Lady Augusta was a Fane on her mother's side, and originally, the house was left jointly to her and her brother, the present Duke of Stanford. Fifteen years ago, Lady Augusta and the duke had a falling out. The upshot was that Lady Augusta instructed me to rent out her half. She moved to Cornwall and not once returned to town."

Nell frowned. "Do I understand you correctly, sir? I must share the house with the Duke of Stanford?"

"Not at all, Miss Hetherington. Lady Augusta had a wall erected to divide the structure into two equal parts, and the double doors of the front entrance have been rebuilt into two separate doors. Your half of the house is Number Two-A, Chandos Street. Number Two is occupied by the duke's grandson, Lady Augusta's great-nephew."

Nell's brow smoothed. "I suppose," she said, looking thoughtful, "Chandos Street is a fashionable address?"

"Indeed. It's just off Cavendish Square. And now, if you'll be kind enough to pour me another glass of port, my dear young lady, we must discuss what you wish to be done about the house."

She nodded and reached for the decanter. *I doubt you'll enter into my schemes with enthusiasm, my good sir*, she thought with some amusement.

"The house is rented at present," Mr. Forsythe continued, "but the lease will expire at the end of April. Shall I arrange the sale of the property? I have already had an offer for it.''

"Sell it? Oh, no!'' Nell spilled some of the wine, but paid no heed to the spreading stain on Miss Mofty's lace cloth. "At the end of April, when the academy closes for the summer, I'll terminate my employment. I shall come to London and live in the house.''

A feeling of gloom settled over the solicitor. He had taken an instant liking to this slip of a girl and had been looking forward to sending her a sizable draft after the sale of the house. He cautiously deposited his bulk on the brittle cane-seat of a straight-backed chair. With even greater caution, he took a few sips of the cheap, sour wine before addressing his client again.

"Forgive me, Miss Hetherington, but is that wise? Your mother succumbed to a fever in Portugal. Your father fell at Coruña. I was informed by the War Office that you are quite alone in the world.''

"You have been busy. As has the War Office.''

Bushy gray brows bristled on the solicitor's broad forehead. "I might still be searching for you if a *busy* clerk at the War Office had not finally advised me to seek out Mr. Wicken, your father's batman. It was Wicken who disclosed that he put you on the stagecoach to Bath after the transports from Coruña landed in Portsmouth.''

A smile curved her mouth. Wicken had been more than her father's batman. He had appointed himself her nursemaid and later her groom. That was when the family had still lived in India. In Portugal, after Mama died, he had also been her chaperon and protector, for Papa had been on Sir John Moore's staff and far too busy.

"Dear old Wicken. How is he, Mr. Forsythe? I believed him to be returned to Spain, fighting under Lord Wellington.''

"He planned to.'' Mr. Forsythe finished his wine. "I believe his wound did not heal as it should. Gangrene set in.''

"They''—her tongue stumbled over the awful word—"amputated? But it was only a minor wound. A mere scratch.''

"Happens all the time, my dear. I suspect it wasn't

cleaned properly aboard the vessel. And when he was admitted to the hospital, it was too late to stave off the infection." The solicitor looked at her curiously. "Why did you pick Bath, of all places?"

"My mother often spoke of Miss Mofty, who, before she established her own school here in Bath, was Mother's governess. I hoped Miss Mofty would recommend me to some genteel family."

"*You* were planning to become a governess?"

Nell chuckled. "Miss Mofty sounded just as incredulous. I promise you, though, I deal very well with the young ladies here at the academy. They have learned to respect me, despite my lack of inches."

"My dear Miss Hetherington, I do not doubt that you're an excellent teacher."

"I may not have many qualifications to boast of," Nell admitted, "but I am a proficient linguist, you must know. I am fluent in French, German, Spanish, and Portuguese, with a smattering of Italian and Urdu thrown in. Not," she added with an impish grin, "that Urdu is of any use to me in Bath."

"And neither will Urdu be of use in London." Mr. Forsythe regarded her sternly. "Besides, you're far too young to live alone. Properly speaking, you should have a guardian."

Nell raised her chin. Her face, which moments ago had looked young and soft and very vulnerable, mirrored a proud and independent spirit. "I shall be twenty come September, and I shan't be living alone in London."

"Miss Hetherington, I cannot advise strongly enough against your move to town. How will you support yourself?"

She smiled, but that quite failed to soothe the solicitor's misgivings. Her next words only increased his gloomy feelings.

"Mr. Forsythe," Elinor Christina Hetherington said calmly. "I can support myself. I know exactly what I want to do with the house."

Chapter Two

May, 1811

Deverell Mackenzie Fenton, Marquis of Ellsworth, whistled as he guided his curricle out of the lantern-lit yard of the Green Man in Barnet. The last stage before London. If the team proved as good as the ostler had promised, he'd be in Josephine's bed before midnight.

Josephine. That delicious bit of French fluff. She had cost him dearly since he had installed her in Great-Aunt Augusta's part of the house. First, there had been the outrageously costly lease; then, Josephine had demanded a phaeton and pair; and finally, there were the jewels, gowns, and innumerable "small necessities," all of which had amounted to three thousand pounds in the twelvemonth he had known her.

But she was worth every penny.

Dev stopped whistling. Four and a half months was a long time to neglect one's mistress. Too long. He'd be treated to a fine display of her volatile Gallic temperament.

He flicked the reins. Instantly the team picked up speed. The curricle, built to his own specifications, swayed precariously as the horses swept around a bend. A slight cough beside him reminded Dev of his groom's presence, but he did not check the wild pace. Mayhap it was madness to race at night, but there was a bit of moonlight and he knew this stretch of road as well as he knew the curves of Josephine's body.

With every passing mile, Dev felt slip away some of the

fatigue and soreness his body had stored up during the long journey from Scotland. His anticipation mounted. By the time he reached London he could taste Josephine's skin, smell her perfume. He sent the curricle rattling along the cobbled streets toward the fashionable west end of town. He sped down Chandos Street, almost to the corner of Cavendish Square, then reined in. Before the carriage had come to a complete stop, he tossed the reins to his long-suffering groom, jumped to the ground, and ran up the steps to Number Two.

Dev cast a speculative glance at the door of Number Two-A, not eighteen inches away from his own front door. He could easily vault the low wrought-iron railing separating him from the other side—Josephine's side—but she was a fastidious woman, his French mistress. She would not welcome him in all his dirt, and he must be at pains to keep Josephine complaisant. She'd have to move if he and his grandfather succeeded in buying Number Two-A from Augusta's heir. Josephine wouldn't like it, but it was dashed bad *ton* to have one's mistress under one's own roof.

If the solicitor ever found the heir.

Dev stepped into his own narrow vestibule. A small lamp burned low on a shelf beside the hall mirror, and Salcombe, the octogenarian butler he had inherited from his older brother, Edward, along with the residence at Number Two, Chandos Street, greeted him with barely concealed satisfaction.

"I reckoned you wouldn't arrive on the morrow like you wrote, my lord, traveling in the chaise with your valet and outriders," the spindly retainer said.

Dev grinned. "Too slow by half, Salcombe, and I am three days late as it is. Any message from my grandfather?"

The butler received the marquis's dust-covered driving coat and the tall beaver hat that had covered his unruly chestnut hair. "His Grace was in town last month, my lord. He left a note. Shall I fetch it?"

The clock in Dev's study at the end of the hallway chimed twelve times. "No," he said. "Let it wait until the morrow. If it had been urgent, my grandfather would undoubtedly have sent for me in Scotland. What I need now is a bath."

"Ben waited up to carry your bathwater, my lord, and

Mrs. Ingles had me take a cold collation to your room afore she retired.''

"Thank you, Salcombe. You may go to bed now." Taking the stairs two steps at a time, Dev raced up to the second floor.

A half hour later, knotting the belt of his brocaded dressing robe around his waist, he moved silently through the dark house. He needed no light; his slippered feet were familiar with every step he made along the corridors, down the stairs, through the kitchen, and into the cellars. As he passed the racks holding his store of port and Madeira, he slowed down, stretching one arm out in front of him until his fingers touched the rough wooden slats of a door.

Dev snatched a key from the pocket of his dressing robe. He swore softly when he missed the lock on the first try. Finally the door creaked open, and Dev stepped into the neighboring cellars.

He moved swiftly now, consumed by impatience. Up the flight of stone steps into Josephine's kitchen quarters, up the stairs to the entrance hall. Here, too, everything was steeped in darkness. Yet Dev made no use of a candle, although he knew that several would be reposing on the buhl table between the parlor and the dining room doors. He knew his way. This vestibule was the mirror image of his own. The stairs leading to Josephine's third-floor bedroom were the other half of his own stairs; they'd been divided by a solid brick wall ever since his grandfather and Augusta had quarreled.

Tugging on the belt of his dressing robe, Dev sped upstairs. He rounded the newel post on the first-floor landing and was about to tackle the next flight when his toes crashed into something rock solid.

"Hell and damnation!" Dev came to an abrupt halt. He shook off his slipper and gingerly touched his smarting foot.

Still standing on one foot, he listened. Nothing stirred upstairs. Josephine had ever been a sound sleeper.

Cautiously, Dev reinserted his foot in the slipper, then bent to explore the obstruction that had caused his agony. Encountering smooth wood and sharp metal corners, he swore again.

Trunks. Three of them. If that didn't cool his ardor,

nothing would. Josephine was moving out. His four-month absence had been too long. Even now she might be upstairs with her new protector.

"Bloody hell! I'm still paying the rent and the bills," he muttered. "I'll toss him out on his ear."

His sore toes forgotten, Dev dashed up to the second floor, then, as he reached the third, he slowed to a more cautious pace. No point bursting into Josephine's chamber like an enraged bull. He might, after all, be mistaken.

His pride told him he *must* be mistaken.

Carefully avoiding the center of the topmost steps, which had a tendency to creak, Dev approached the door opposite the stairway. His hand curled around the handle and pressed down. The door opened without sound or resistance. For an instant he was confused. There should have been a mouselike squeak.

The soft rustle of sheets and feather quilts recalled his mind to more pressing matters. Josephine. Alone, if he judged correctly by the stillness in the chamber.

His mouth curled in a satisfied smile as he prowled toward the bed. He could see a cascade of hair against the white pillows, and felt the familiar stirring of desire. Josephine had always, instantly, aroused his passion.

A shrug of his shoulders, and his dressing robe slid to the ground. He kicked off his slippers. Clad only in a pair of knit pantaloons, Dev lowered himself onto the bed. Unerringly, his mouth found its target just behind her ear, beneath the silken strands of hair. His hand cupped delicious softness.

Softness shrouded in thick flannel.

Nell jerked awake.

Her breast was on fire, as was her neck. A scream rose in her throat. She bit it back. Papa did not care for screaming. He'd send her to England if she could not bear up like a soldier.

But Papa was dead, and so was Sir John Moore, and many, many more. And she was in England. In London, in her own house.

"Who the devil are you?" a deep voice demanded furiously. Gripping her shoulder, the intruder in her bed sat up. "And where is Josephine?"

Nell paid scant attention. Let him ask questions, as many

as he pleased. She groped under her pillows for the silver-mounted handle of the small gun Papa had given her for her sixteenth birthday.

There. Her fingers clutched the weapon. She flung herself around and fired blindly in the direction of that deep voice just as the bruising hand on her shoulder started to shake her like a rag doll.

A shower of plaster from the ceiling made her sneeze, and then she held the pistol no more. The intruder had wrested it from her.

Nell screamed. Instantly, a dark shadow loomed above her. A cuff to her jaw set her ears ringing, but it promptly stilled her outburst of hysteria.

"Save the Cheltenham tragedy," the man said brusquely.

Again she was seized, this time to be dragged off the bed and propped like a useless broom against the wall between the two bedroom windows.

"I don't mean you any harm, girl." The low voice sounded resigned now, no longer furious, and there was something disturbingly familiar about it. "I'll light a candle if only you'll remain still for a moment."

She sensed that he was looking at her, waiting for her reply.

Nell swallowed. "Yes. I'll be still."

He released her. Turning away, he muttered, "Trust a female to fly off the handle for no reason at all. Damn, but if they aren't a nuisance. Every single one of them."

Nell gasped as she remembered the voice and similar words uttered three long years ago. She remembered her mad gallop to the front of the straggling English troops crossing Portugal. The dust, the parching sun. . . . She had to get to her father, to tell him that Mama had succumbed to her illness.

A French infantry regiment had attacked. Grapeshot and shells were bursting all around, peppering her with dirt and fragments of rock and metal. Her mount reared. Someone dragged her off the horse, pinned her to the ground. She screamed, but a firm mouth pressed against hers, silencing her.

"Trust a female to fly off the handle when you want to save her," the young officer had grumbled when he finally released her mouth. He had lost his shako, and his chestnut hair had gleamed with streaks of reddish gold in the bright Portuguese sun. "What a nuisance you are. Pluck up, Nell! It's naught but a skirmish."

She had met Devil Mackenzie many times before. After all, he had been one of her father's officers, but he had never smiled at her like that, disarming, devastating. He had plumb knocked the breath out of her. His eyes, a warm, deep dark blue, the color of the Indian sky she had left behind, had danced with a merriment that had made her heart turn somersaults. . . .

Nell's shoulders slumped against her bedroom wall as she heard him fumble with the matches and the tinderbox on her bedside table. She should have recognized his voice with the first word he uttered. How fickle youthful love was.

"There now," he said, turning up the wick of the old-fashioned oil lamp. "Isn't that better?"

"Devil Mackenzie." Nell straightened and stepped into the circle of light. "*Nothing* will make this situation any better."

Fascinated, she watched his brows climb until they threatened to disappear in the shock of hair falling onto his forehead.

"Nell!" he said, incredulous. "Jack Hetherington's pesky brat. What the devil are you doing in Josephine's house?"

She stiffened, every vestige of that old infatuation torn from her heart by his words. "It is *my* house. What are *you* doing here, Devil Mackenzie?"

"Dammit," Dev said, grinning down at her, "if it doesn't take one back. It's been years since anyone addressed me by that name."

"You didn't answer my question. What are you doing here?" *And who the devil is Josephine?*

"You haven't changed. Or, maybe," he said, considering, "just a little. Your skin has a more ladylike hue. You've filled out in certain places, but you haven't added an inch to your height, and your hair still tumbles around you like a lion's mane. How old are you now, brat? Eighteen?"

Nell drew herself up. "I was going on eighteen when

you last saw me. I am almost twenty, Lieutenant Fenton. Hardly of an age to be called 'brat.' "

"*Almost* twenty. My felicitations, Miss Hetherington." He presented her with a mock bow. "And as you have passed the brat stage I no longer am Lieutenant Fenton. Behold, the Marquis of Ellsworth. But you may call me Dev."

He stepped closer. Instinctively, Nell retreated. She drew in her breath sharply as the warm glow of the lamp fell on the matting of tight chestnut-colored curls covering his upper torso. His slim hips and muscular thighs were accentuated by skintight knit pantaloons.

And she in her nightgown.

"My lord! This is hardly the time or place for a renewal of our acquaintance. I suggest that you dress and leave this house immediately. You may call on me in the morning."

"It is morning." He bent to retrieve his dressing robe. Slipping his arms into the brocaded material, he grinned. "There now. I'm dressed."

"You came—" She imagined him striding through the streets in his exotic robe, and words failed her. Devil Mackenzie had turned into a lunatic.

A silvery gleam on the carpet caught her eye. While Dev was tying the belt of his robe, Nell pushed past him. She picked up her pistol and leveled it at his chest.

"Go," she commanded. "Now!"

Again she watched the steady climb of his brows. The corners of his mouth twitched. "As you wish, Miss Hetherington. I shall do myself the honor of calling on you at a more convenient time."

"At a more conventional time," she corrected him. Any time would be better than now, if, indeed, he dared return. In a few hours Wicken would be here. He would know how to deal with unwelcome callers.

Nell picked up the lamp and followed Dev as he sauntered out into the hallway, making his way leisurely down the stairs. Her father had often bragged about Devil Mackenzie, his coolness and levelheadedness under fire. She had proof of it now. Few men would be calm with a pistol pointed at their backs. A pistol held by a woman who had to kick aside the folds of her nightgown before she could venture a step.

"How did you get in?" she asked sharply. "If you broke a window——" The expense would ruin her. Her pockets would soon be to-let, and she must still purchase so many items.

"I am not a housebreaker. What a poor opinion you must have of me."

She heard the amusement in his voice. Well, it would be she who'd laugh when he found himself in the street in his dressing robe.

But when they descended to the vestibule, Devil Mackenzie passed the front door. Nell hurried to catch up with him as he followed the hallway to the back stairs and carefully made his way down the steep, narrow steps. He finally stopped before the cellar door and turned with a grin.

"No need to come any farther. There might be mice and rats, and I don't care to be thought callous for leaving a swooning female behind while I make my getaway."

"No fear of that, my lord. You, however, may find yourself at point nonplus when I turn the key behind you."

He laughed. Touching two fingers to his tousled locks in a casual salute, he opened the door and disappeared down into the dark cellars.

Nell realized then that she would find a door below, connecting her half with that of Number Two. Hampered by the pistol in one hand and the lamp in the other, Nell hesitated. She had not examined the cellars when she moved in the day before, deeming it unnecessary to venture into that realm of cobwebs and spiders—and rats and mice. But she must bar that door.

She lowered her pistol and grabbed a fold of her nightgown, hitching it off the floor. "You are Lady Augusta's great-nephew," she called out accusingly, as she forged down the cold, dank steps.

And Josephine was his mistress, the tenant whom Mr. Forsythe had such trouble evicting.

The light of her lantern fell on Dev, standing in an open doorway. Beyond the door stretched rack upon rack of dusty bottles. He looked at her over his shoulder, and she could see his devilish grin.

"Next time you threaten an intruder with a gun," he

said, "make certain you reload after firing a shot. Good night, Miss Hetherington."

The door closed in her face. She heard a key turn, heard his soft laughter, then silence.

Nell looked down at the pistol clutched among several folds of flannel in her hand. Her face flamed with chagrin. Her mouth tightened, then, reluctantly, curved into a smile.

Round one to you, my lord marquis, but you shan't catch me off-guard again.

Chapter Three

"There must be *something* we can do, Wicken."

Nell raised her lantern and frowned at the empty flour barrel she had pushed in front of the cellar door after Devil Mackenzie had disappeared through it in the middle of the night. "Nail it shut?" she said doubtfully.

"Nails won't hold, but I'll find something heavier than this flimsy barrel." Wicken, short and wiry, scratched the stump of his left arm. The empty sleeve came untucked from his coat pocket. Impatiently, he stuffed it back in. "Reckon we could get a stone mason to sink an anchor for a bolt, Miss Nell. Nothin' else we can do since the door opens our way."

"Drat! As though I had money to fritter away." Nell spun on her heel. "Leave it for now," she said, climbing the steep, curving steps to the kitchen. "We'll lock the door up here."

Wicken followed, peering at her from under knit brows. "Never say ye're afeared of the lieutenant. He may be a wild 'un, but the major thought the world of him."

"Naturally Papa would see no wrong in Devil Mackenzie. He and the lieutenant were two of a kind. Besides," Nell added, shutting the cellar door, "he's an officer no longer. He is now the Marquis of Ellsworth."

"I heard tell that he first lost his father and then his older brother in some pestilent epidemic, and that's how he got his title. Heir to the Duke of Stanford he is. Still, I knew him as Lieutenant Fenton, and that's the name as sticks to mind."

Wicken saw Nell struggle with the rusty key in the cellar door. He took it from her. "I'll see to the lock."

"Confound it! Everything is falling to rack and ruin. I spent an hour yesterday greasing door hinges and stiff windows."

"Mind yer language, Miss Nell." Wicken adopted the stern-father tone he had employed with her ever since she, as a three-year-old in Bengal, had dazzled him with her bright, impish smile. A rare handful Miss Nell had been and, no doubt, still was. He had set foot into this sliver of a house no more than a couple of hours ago, and already he had figured out that she was knee-deep into one of her madcap schemes.

Nudging her toward the stove, he said, "You be a good girl 'n put the kettle on for a nice cup o' tea. Been worritin' too much, ye have. But now, Wicken is here to look after ye."

A smile lurked in her eyes. "Have you changed your mind, then? You're not going to wash your hands of me, dear Wicken? I was afraid I had really done it this time. You looked fit to burst when I told you about my school."

Clamping the key under the stub of his arm, Wicken scraped the rusty metal with his fingernail. "Dumbfool notion if ye ask me," he muttered. "But, of course, ye didn't ask anyone."

From her small store, Nell carefully measured tea into an earthenware pot. "Now who was it?" she mused. "In Bangalore, I believe . . . someone grumbled about green

English brides, who stirred up more trouble than a herd of stampeding elephants.''

''Aye,'' Wicken shot back, ''but I never rec'mended that a stampeding ellyphant should teach those brides how to behave in India.''

Nell chuckled. ''Surely I was not *that* wild. Here, drink your tea. I'm going upstairs to test the targets.''

''Don't touch them new pistols until I check 'em over.'' Wicken deftly applied oil to the key, then inserted it in the lock. It turned smoothly.

''And let me have a peep at yer own pistol, Miss Nell!'' he called out as she carried her cup from the kitchen.

Nell winced. If it came to Wicken's ears that she had forgotten to reload her weapon after firing, she'd never hear the end of it. She could only pray that Devil Mackenzie was gentleman enough to keep silent about her slip.

Stopping on the first floor to take a sip of her tea, she peeked into the drawing room. The hands of the ormolu clock atop the fireplace mantel showed a quarter past eleven. Surely a good time for a morning call. Dev had promised—or threatened—to call again.

Perhaps he was descending his part of the stairs behind the bricks even now, as she was going up. Nell tried to imagine him, dressed to the nines like the dandies she had encountered on her one brief sojourn to Bond Street. He'd be wearing a brocaded vest, a coat padded in the shoulders and nipped in at the waist, his stiff shirt-points and intricately tied cravat holding up his chin.

Chuckling, Nell entered the bedroom farthest removed from the dividing wall. Try as she might, she could not picture him other than in his trim, crimson field-tunic.

Or bare-chested, muscles rippling in the soft glow of an oil lamp.

With more force than was good for it, she set her teacup onto the windowsill, then strode to the south wall of the apartment, the only wall without windows or a door. She and Wicken had spent the better part of an hour nailing thick quilts to the oaken paneling. Atop the quilts they had started to tack various targets: life-size drawings of snakes found in India, a tiger's head with fangs bared in a vicious snarl, several wafers with black circles whose bull's-eyes were marked in crimson.

She was hammering a tack through the tiger's left eye when Wicken joined her. "I don't like this, Miss Nell," he said. "Not one bit. Target practice is an outdoor sport, an' you'll not convince me otherwise."

"I know," she said patiently for the seventh or eighth time that morning. "And I hate to ruin good paneling, but you saw the garden behind the house. Barely large enough to hold a cluster of ferns, and the wall around it only waist-high. More than likely my students would hit the Marquis of Ellsworth rather than my targets. Not that he doesn't deserve it, mind you, but think of the scandal it would create."

"Now, Miss Nell," Wicken expostulated, but before he could deliver a full-fledged scold, the sound of the door knocker drove him from the room.

"If it is the marquis," Nell called after him, "don't, for goodness sake, bring him up here or to the second floor. I'll see him in the drawing room."

Muttering unintelligibly, Wicken hurried downstairs. The knocker sounded again, more demanding. He clutched at the stub of his arm. *Dang it!* He'd eat his empty sleeve if they weren't in for a change of weather. Most likely cold and rain if the burning and throbbing of his lost limb were anything to go by.

"Hold yer horses!" he shouted when the raps on the front door were repeated a third time. "I'm acomin'!"

As fast as his short, bandied legs would carry him, he rushed down the last flight of stairs. He flung open the door, and his scowl vanished. A wide gap-toothed smile spread over his weathered countenance. "Lieutenant Fenton! Ye're a sight for sore eyes, sir."

Grinning, Dev shook hands with Major Hetherington's former batman. "So the Frenchies didn't get you after all. Should have known you were too wily and tough for them."

"'Tween't for the lack of trying that they didn't catch me. Had to make do with a piece of me arm, though. Step inside, Lieutenant. My lord, I should say."

Dev set his hat and gloves onto the buhl table. "So you're still looking after the major's pesky brat?"

"Aye." A look of reproof came to Wicken's eyes. "And it appears I should've been here last night," he said sternly.

"A misunderstanding, Wicken. It shan't happen again, I promise you." Dev cocked his head in the direction of the stairs. "Will she see me, do you think?"

"She'll see ye. Told me to show ye into the drawing room." Wicken hesitated, then said, "Last night ye didn't come knockin' on the front door. Ye came sneakin' through the cellars. It weren't right, Lieutenant."

One foot on the stairs, Dev stopped and looked back at the older man. "I believed myself to be the lessee of this house. You can, perhaps, imagine my chagrin when I read my mail this morning and found a letter from Miss Nell's solicitor, canceling the lease as of four days ago."

For a moment longer, Wicken held the marquis's steady gaze, then, moving toward the back of the foyer, said, "I'll fetch a glass of somethin'. No doubt you'll need it when Miss Nell is through with ye. And no doubt ye know yer way to the drawing room."

"No doubt, indeed."

Dev had reached the first-floor landing and was about to enter the drawing room when the sound of quick, light footsteps drew his eyes to the stairway leading to the upper floors. He was aware that he was goggling, but couldn't help himself.

The diminutive young lady coming down the stairs, her tawny hair brushed toward her right ear and confined in one long braid, was a vision to knock the breath out of the most blasé connoisseur of femininity. A length of soft, airy cotton cloth, cunningly pleated in the front to allow for an easy stride, wrapped her hips and legs, then, not unlike a Scottish plaid, it draped her bosom and left shoulder, revealing her bare right forearm and a bit of cotton sleeve, the same brilliant peacock blue as her exotic overgarment.

"Do you like my sari, my lord?" Wide gray eyes unblinkingly met his astonished gaze. She paused on the second-to-last step, one hand on the baluster, the other raising the folds of the sari to allow a glimpse of bare toes peeping from a dainty sandal. "Shocking, isn't it?"

Nell's smile stirred memories of the impish child he had

known in the Peninsula. He couldn't help but smile back. "Let's say unexpected."

"As is *your* apparel," she said, minutely examining his riding coat, his buckskin breeches and shining Hessians. "Where is your quizzing glass, my lord? Where are the falls of lace at wrist and throat, the fobs and seals, the gold or silver tassels on your boots?"

"You'll not catch me decked out like a Bond Street beau." He stepped toward her, his hand extended. "Come on down, Nell. I must speak with you."

She allowed herself to be ushered into the drawing room before saying, "Yes, I believe you owe me an explanation. Possibly an apology?"

Dev caught her sidelong look at him as she seated herself on one of the cherry-wood chairs, relics from Lady Augusta's days. He frowned at the chintz covers, which stood in dire need of refurbishing—as they had when Josephine banished the chairs into the attic and teased him to purchase a set of low couches in the Egyptian style, as expensive as they were uncomfortable.

Josephine—it was because of her that he found himself in the unenviable position of having to beg Nell's pardon. And Nell a slip of a girl whom years ago he had held by the scruff of her neck, shaking her until her teeth rattled. She should count herself lucky that he hadn't blistered her backside, for she'd had the unmitigated gall to take out one of his best horses and, on a dare, had raced against Cyprian Westcott across the rough Portuguese terrain.

"The chairs are quite sturdy," said Nell, regarding his murderous scowl with fascination. "Please sit down."

He ignored her invitation, striding instead to the fireplace where he propped a shoulder against the jutting mantelshelf. He transferred his frown to her, but still did not speak.

"It goes against the grain to apologize, doesn't it, my lord?"

"I told you to call me Dev." His brow cleared, and the tightness around his mouth disappeared as one corner twitched suspiciously. "We're far too intimately acquainted to stand on ceremony. After all—"

"Quite so," she interrupted hastily. It would be just like

Devil Mackenzie to remind her *how* he knew her intimately. "If you like, we'll forget all about last night and start afresh."

"It'll be impossible to forget last night, my dear Nell."

"Oh? I thought it would be nothing out of the ordinary for you to find yourself escorted from a lady's bedchamber. Although, I imagine, in the general run of things it would have been the lady's husband who pointed the gun at your head."

"My back, dear Nell. You pointed the gun at my back. Unloaded, too."

"I wonder you didn't take it from me."

"I couldn't. The pain in my toes was killing me."

Her startled gaze flew to the tips of his gleaming Hessians. "I thought I hit the ceil—dash it! You're hoaxing me."

"Not at all. I injured my toes on one of those infernal trunks you've stored on the landing. I say, Nell, you can't be much of a housekeeper if you don't know that trunks ought to be stashed away in the attics or in the cellar."

"I certainly could use them in the cellar since I don't have a key to lock the door leading to your part of the house."

"I plumb forgot." With an engaging grin, Dev pushed away from the fireplace and started to turn out his pockets. "No great wonder, though. You quite bowled me over with that costume of yours. Planning to go to a masquerade, are you?"

"Stupid," she said crossly. "A sari looks much better on a short lady than does a high-waisted muslin gown with flounced hem and a sash—"

"Makes you look like a child dressed up in her mama's gown, doesn't it? Ah! Here it is." Bowing with inimitable grace, Dev handed her a large brass key.

"Thank you." Her annoyance with him forgotten, Nell said quizzingly, "How trusting Mademoiselle Josephine was."

"Impertinent chit," he muttered, inserting his muscular frame gingerly into one of the cherry-wood chairs.

"Tell me, Dev. Why did you pay me, or rather my house, a visit last night? Surely you were aware that Josephine departed when her lease expired."

"It was *my* lease," he said in clipped tones, "and I was *not* aware that it had not been renewed."

"Tut, tut." Nell placed the key atop a small marquetry table at her elbow. "You can't be much of a provider when you allow such an important date to slip your mind."

Dev shot her a dagger-look but said with admirable calm, "I'll thank you not to speak on subjects of which you cannot possibly have knowledge."

"Fustian! Don't be so stuffy, Dev."

"Why, you brat!"

A flush of dull red spread over his tanned face. Nell did not mistake it for a blush of embarrassment. She steeled herself for a thundering scold, but when he spoke, it was in quite a mild tone of voice, and once more she had to admire his self-control.

"Let's get down to the point of my visit."

"*This* visit, or last night's?" she murmured, absorbed in the contemplation of his hand atop the armrest of the chair. It was a shapely hand, as bronzed as his face, with long fingers and carefully buffed nails. Only the sudden show of whiteness around the knuckles intimated that he had heard her words.

"I have come, Nell, to make you an offer for this house."

She looked up in astonishment. "What makes you think I'd want to sell?"

He raised a brow. "It takes funds to maintain an establishment in town. When Mr. Forsythe informed my grandfather and me of Augusta's death and the bequest of her London house to her goddaughter, he made no mention of a monetary provision."

"You forget that I also inherited from my parents."

His other brow rose as well. "*You* forget that I was well acquainted with your father. I doubt you inherited anything but debts."

"How . . . low!" Nell's eyes flashed angrily. "And I thought you liked Papa!"

"Take a damper, Nell. Of course I liked Jack. All of us did." In fact, the seasoned campaigner had been like a father to the raw young officers assigned to Sir John Moore. Dev had been one of them. He had just turned four-and-twenty when he arrived in Portugal. But no one knew better than he that Jack was a gamester. Jack would bet on anything.

"Do you remember Salamanca, Nell? When Moore learned that the French were closer to us than either Baird's or Hope's troops, and he ordered the women to stay behind? Well, your father gave me odds that you'd find a way to continue with us."

Nell blushed, remembering the two weeks she had spent as Sir John Moore's own "mess boy," wearing breeches, a baggy coat, and a tattered shako. Sir John had paid no attention to the "boy" who served his meals, but Devil Mackenzie and his friends had recognized her instantly and teased her unmercifully.

"It just serves to show," she said, pointing her nose in the air, "that Papa was not one to lose his bets."

Dev laughed, and Nell, hearing Wicken's footsteps in the corridor, hurried to open the door. Dev had an excellent view of her angrily swaying hips, and if she had been wearing anything but a sari he might have accused her of flouncing to the door.

Wicken, balancing in his right hand a tarnished salver with two glasses, advanced toward Dev. "So ye're still here," he said with satisfaction. "Miss Nell told ye what she plans to do?"

"No, and I'm not sure I wish to know. I offered to buy this house. It would please my grandfather no end if it were restored to the family. With Augusta dead, he feels honor bound to tear down the dividing wall."

"Best thing I've heard yet," muttered Wicken. "With the money this house'll bring, you'll be settled snug, Miss Nell."

"Oh, shush!" Nell resumed her seat and looked curiously at Dev. "Why did your grandfather and my godmother quarrel?"

"I couldn't begin to guess," Dev said in a bored voice. "Some old scandal, no doubt." He took one of the glasses Wicken offered, swirling the contents gently under his nose. "I say!" he exclaimed. "This is dashed good brandy."

Nell threw Wicken a glance of reproach but continued

to address Dev. "If there had been a scandal, surely you would know of it."

"I don't. Must have been hushed up. Grandfather won't talk about Augusta, and I only have the observations of a twelve-year-old from which to draw conclusions. Not very reliable, you must admit."

Nell sampled the brandy, threw Wicken another glance that promised he hadn't heard the last about serving the good brandy, then said, "I wish I had thought of seeking out my godmother after Coruña, but since we never received letters from her, and Miss Mofty, on the other hand, was a regular correspondent, it simply didn't occur to me. I do remember, though, that my mother once termed her a dashing lady with rather advanced ideas."

Dev met Nell's questioning look with a wide grin. "I doubt not that your mother was right. Augusta was much younger than Grandfather. I recall her as a beautiful woman, fluttering from one ball to the next, always at odds with the family, who believed she should be wearing black gloves for old Fawnhope. Augusta, you see, was convinced that three months was long enough to mourn her spouse."

"That might account for the wall."

"And now," said Wicken, purposefully steering the conversation back to what he considered the main point, "ye're wishful of tearing it down. A good thing, too, if I may say so, Lieutenant. How much of the ready are ye willing to offer Miss Nell?"

Dev named a sum that made Nell gasp, while Wicken gave a low whistle through the gap in his teeth. For a long, painful moment, Nell stared at the key on the table beside her. Wisely invested, the money would keep her in comfort for the rest of her life. She could buy a cozy little cottage in some quiet country town and employ a maid servant to do the work, and as a sop to the proprieties.

It would be hard, though—perhaps impossible—to convince Wicken that she still needed him when she could afford to pay for the services of an able-bodied man.

And she would surely die of boredom in a little country cottage.

Nell rose, holding out her hand to Dev. "Thank you

for your most obliging offer, my lord, but I won't sell the house.''

"Rubbish!" Ignoring her hand, Dev stood up to face her. "Of course you'll sell. You must. Who ever heard of a young girl living alone in town, with only her father's batman for protection!"

He towered head and shoulders above her, and to Nell it seemed as though he were prepared to fight her as determinedly as he had battled the French troops under Marshal Soult at Coruña. Devil Mackenzie was a formidable enemy. Fearless, daring, and untiring.

Unconsciously, she squared her shoulders as she looked up to meet fierce, deep blue eyes. She need not fear him— he was not her enemy, was he?

Behind her back, the fingers of her left hand crossed. "I shan't live alone, my lord. I have asked a friend to live with me and lend me countenance. A most respectable widow.''

"Aye," interjected Wicken, with a fixed stare at Nell's left hand. "It's a pity, it is, that she couldn't move in at the same time *you* did, Miss Nell.''

Dev watched her through narrowed eyes. "And how will you support yourself?''

"I shall open an academy.''

"Miss Nell's Select Academy," offered Wicken.

Incredulous, Dev looked from one to the other. "You'll have scrubby little schoolroom misses traipsing up and down Chandos Street? Giggling and chattering, practically on my doorstep?''

"You are mistaken, my lord," Nell said cooly. "My students will be Young Brides of His Majesty's Officers.''

Chapter Four

Dev stared at Nell, his mind reeling. He remembered her in the Peninsula, a skinny girl huddled under her cloak in a streaming rain while she struggled with flint and kindling to light her father's camp fire. He remembered her pinched nostrils and clenched teeth as she plucked and cleaned a chicken given to her by a Portuguese peasant. And he remembered the flash of anger in her wide gray eyes when someone made the mistake of offering her assistance.

By no means had Nell been the only female capable of looking after herself during that grueling trek across Portugal and Spain, but she had certainly been the only one determined to do so at *all* times. "Just let her have her head," the late Jack Hetherington would advise his fellow officers when they suggested that his daughter's independence and stubbornness might lead her into trouble. "My Nell will come to no harm."

Which was all very well, thought Dev, still slightly dazed, but if she were allowed to have her head in town, there was no telling what might happen.

He shot a glance at Wicken but received no help from that quarter. The batman, his back turned on both Nell and Dev, had replaced the two brandy glasses on the salver and was absorbed in the task of lifting the tray. Dev moved toward the one-armed man but caught himself. He did not need Nell's warning tug on his sleeve or the shake of her head to tell him that Wicken would not thank him for any assistance.

Nell walked to the door, the folds of her sari swaying gracefully about her ankles. "Cat got your tongue? How unusual for Devil Mackenzie. But you'll have to excuse me now. I must see to a thousand-and-one important matters."

"Stay!" Dev caught her in the doorway and pulled her aside to allow Wicken to pass.

"Nell, you cannot do this," he said with authority. "If you want to teach officers' brides, you should rent a house in the country. This is *Fane House*. Augusta would turn in her grave if she knew of your intentions."

Smiling up into his face, she shrugged off his hands. "This, my lord, is *Hetherington House*, and I may do as I please. My plans don't include a retired life in the country. I want to see plays, visit the opera. And above all," she said, her eyes and voice softening, "I want to be where I might meet old friends when they come home on leave."

Dev was not immune to wistfulness. "If that is your ambition, then let me buy this house and you can settle in Hans Town or off Oxford Street where you won't set up your neighbors' backs," he suggested reasonably. "The Dowager Countess of Lansdowne will make it impossible for you to enter society if you start a school on her doorstep."

"No, is she my neighbor?" asked Nell. "I must be sure to call on her. Papa was her favorite whist partner when she visited in India."

"You have an answer for everything." Dev's eyes narrowed. "But let me warn you, brat. You had far better sell the house to me, or at least let me rent it—"

"Stuff!" Nell interrupted. "So that you may reinstall your Josephine? I have a notion Lady Lansdowne would rather see a bevy of brides or affianced young ladies trot up and down Chandos Street than Josephine's bird-of-paradise friends and their illustrious protectors."

Nell would have backed away when Dev took a step closer, but the door jamb pressed against her spine and cut off a strategic retreat. The only recourse left her was a mocking smile, which, judging by the tight knit of Dev's brows and the whiteness around his mouth, only fanned his anger.

"The first thing Lady Lansdowne will do when she hears you speak," he said menacingly, "is wash your mouth with lye soap, my girl. Without a doubt you're eminently suited to being a camp follower, but you're not fit to instruct gently reared young ladies.''

''Then you had best hurry and warn her to put in a goodly supply of soap. Good day, Dev. You know your way out, don't you?''

Abruptly, he turned away. His glance fell on the three trunks lined up beside the stairway. ''Why are they here?'' he said curtly. ''Are you unpacked yet?''

''They are here because the carter refused to lug them any higher on these narrow stairs. And yes, I am unpacked.''

''I'll send my footmen to store them away.''

She blinked, but said with creditable calm, ''You're very kind.''

He shot her an unreadable look and, without vouchsafing a reply, ran down the stairs. A few moments later, Nell had the satisfaction of hearing the front door close with a resounding slam.

For the next hour, she busied herself on the second floor. The library to the right of the stair well could serve as a study. The adjoining chamber and the spacious room opposite, which ran the full length of the second floor, could, with the addition of some chairs and couches, be transformed into informal classrooms.

Frowning, Nell contemplated the intricate pattern of the dusty parquet floor in the vast apartment—her half of the former ballroom of Fane House, no doubt. And completely useless in its white-blue-and-gilt splendor unless she found some merchant willing to sell her furniture on credit.

After a frugal luncheon of coddled eggs on toast, and a small dish of preserved cherries Wicken had found in the cellar among a welter of empty jars, Nell set out to explore the shops along Oxford Street. She went alone. Overruling his protest that he should accompany her, she sent Wicken to purchase staples and to place orders with the butcher and the greengrocer.

Nell stepped briskly, confident that she was looking her best in a gown of striped jaconet and a tight-fitting green spencer piped in black to match the colors of the dress. Two-inch heels on her half-boots and a high-crowned bonnet gave her that bit of additional height she needed to face with confidence the various clutch-fisted shopkeepers she might encounter. Nor would she allow herself to be put out of countenance by raised brows directed at her from elegant ladies walking in twos and threes or with their maids, or by the quizzing glasses leveled at her by beaux and dandies on the strut.

With many a curious peep at such treasures as hats, gloves, and gowns displayed in the show windows, Nell approached the linen warehouse at the corner of Orchard Street, where Miss Mofty had commissioned supplies ever since she established her academy in Bath.

Nell did not envision boarding any of her prospective students, but, on the other hand, it would not do to be caught lacking the necessities. Only a small number of sheets and towels, all threadbare and mended and bearing the initial *F*, had been left behind by Josephine. Lady Augusta Fawnhope's property, Nell suspected. It had probably survived from the days when Lady Augusta's mother had still been a Fane.

Mr. Soames, the proprietor of the warehouse, received Nell politely, if with reserve. He peered around and behind her, adjusting his gold-rimmed spectacles repeatedly as though hopeful of seeing a maid, if only he could position his glasses just right. When she stated her requirements, he beckoned a hovering clerk and retreated, obviously deeming it below his dignity to serve such an insignificant customer himself.

Nell soon completed her purchases. "I am Miss Elinor Hetherington," she told the clerk. "You may have the items delivered later this afternoon at Number Two-A, Chandos Street."

"Well, I don't know, miss," the clerk said haughtily. "We generally deliver large orders only."

Mr. Soames appeared at Nell's elbow. Bowing deeply and, at the same time, flicking impatient fingers at the clerk, who had started to write out the bill, he stammered, "Miss, ah, Hetherington? So sorry! Didn't quite realize . . . not until I heard the address that is . . . but of course I'll have the items delivered. At your convenience, miss."

More pleased than surprised, Nell watched the clerk and the bill disappear around some rows of shelves. This was proof that what was needed was only the magic sound of a fashionable address to command exemplary service and instant credit. And this was why she had not wanted Wicken to accompany her. Wicken did not believe in buying on tick.

. She smiled at the linen draper. "I planned to return some other time to look at table linens. But, perhaps, since I am here . . . ?"

"Quite so. It'll be my pleasure, Miss Hetherington."

Mr. Soames placed before her beautiful linen cloths and napkins edged with lace, embroidered cloths, and table cloths of stiff, lustrous damask. Nell chose an Irish linen and a dozen matching napkins, but assured Mr. Soames that she would be back for further selections.

She left the linen draper's well pleased with herself and her purchases. A hackney coach took her to two furniture warehouses recommended by Miss Mofty, and here, too, the mention of her fashionable address served to smooth her path. She came away the proud possessor of eight upholstered chairs, two couches, a half-dozen stools with scrolled feet and caned tops, a medley of small tables, and not so much as a single bill to weigh down her purse.

Her successful expedition left her feeling thrilled and pleasantly tired. She told the jarvey to take her home and was about to climb into the hackney when she was hailed from a high-perch phaeton that pulled up behind.

A small tiger ran to the horses' heads while Devil Mackenzie sprang lightly to the ground. Nell had time only to watch Dev flip a coin to her hackney driver and admire the old man's dexterity catching it in midair before she was tossed into the high seat of the phaeton.

"Well!" she said as Dev climbed up beside her and set his pair of matched bays in motion. "I call this high-handed treatment. A kidnapping, no less!"

"Had to talk with you some more, brat." He shot her a look brimful of mischief. "But didn't want to risk a dismissal like this morning. My compliments on your outfit, by the way. I was wrong. You do not look at all like a child playing at dress-up. You look elegant. And *without*," he marveled, "the assistance of a maid."

"If you plan to read me a lecture on going about without an abigail, save your breath."

"I will. Besides, phaetons aren't built for three."

The carriage whisked into Holborn, and Nell said, studiously avoiding his laughing eyes, "Since I am forced to drive with you, the least you could do is take me to see the sights."

"What sights?" he asked with suspicion.

"St. Paul's, the Tower, Westminster Abbey, the British Museum—"

"Enough!" A shudder ran through his muscular frame. "I'll drive you past some of those edifices, but I'll be dashed if I stop and trudge after you while you poke around inside."

"Some other time, then. What did you wish to speak to me about, Dev?"

He took a moment before replying. "I want to talk about you," he said finally, his attention focused on the horses. "You really mustn't live in London without a chaperon, you know."

She started to protest, but Dev cut her off with an imperative lift of his hand. "My dear Nell, if you think I believed that nonsense about a respectable widow coming to live with you—dash it! You forget I'm familiar with your habit of promising with your fingers crossed behind your back."

"I did no such thing!"

"You did, too. And if you don't watch out, you may find yourself saddled with a strict guardian. You *are* under age, you know."

Mr. Forsythe had said much the same, Nell ruefully recalled.

At that moment the phaeton swung into the dip south on Newgate Street and St. Paul's Cathedral come into view, making, in Nell's opinion, a reply unnecessary. She sat in rapt admiration of Wren's magnificent monument, and it was not until they rattled farther east toward the Tower that she acknowledged the veracity of Dev's statement.

"I was toying with the notion," she said, carefully choosing her words, "of inviting Bess Wainwright to stay with me."

"Perfect," Dev said scathingly. "A scatterbrain if ever I met one."

"She *is* a widow."

"She is also a silly widgeon with the brain of a peahen."

Nell swallowed a retort. He was absolutely right, of course, but unlike Dev she saw nothing wrong in having a silly widgeon for a chaperon. She resolved to write Bess that very night.

"I only wonder you don't suggest I hire a strapping footman or two for my protection."

"Do you now?" Expertly, Dev guided his pair around a string of carts laden with fish, then turned into Tower Street. "But you must know, my dear Nell, that I place full confidence in Wicken's ability to keep intruders at bay. One-armed though he may be, *he* won't neglect to reload his pistol."

"Unfair, Dev! Surely the circumstances of our encounter must excuse my lapse."

"And if all else fails," he continued, "I give you permission to use the cellar door and come to me for protection."

"Thank you. But *your* kind of protection I can do without, Devil Mackenzie."

"Lud, you have a sharp tongue, brat. You need not fear I'd try to seduce you. I like my ladies sweeter-tempered."

Nell darted a glance at him. "Is that what Josephine is? Sweet-tempered? I do believe she threw the fireplace tongs at Mr. Forsythe's clerk when he asked her to vacate the premises."

"He had no business discussing Josephine with you," he said curtly.

Nell ignored the now-familiar signal of his rising temper. "Depend upon it," she said musingly, "Josephine expected you to make certain she wouldn't be evicted. How careless of you to forget the lease. Didn't Mr. Forsythe inform you that I planned to move in?"

"He did. I read his letter and a message to that effect from my grandfather only *after* I invaded your bedchamber."

"I see that I must have speech with Mr. Forsythe. It is insupportable that he did not notify you sooner."

"You know very well that he did. I admit the fault is mine for staying on in Scotland and not having my post sent on to me. I apologize. There, does that satisfy you, brat?"

"Completely. Did it satisfy Josephine?"

"It is a miracle you reached maturity," he said through clenched teeth. "I wonder no one tried to wring your neck."

"*You* tried, after my race with Cyprian Westcott," she reminded him. "I believe you limped for several days."

"You do have a vicious kick," he admitted with reluctance. "Now hush and appreciate. I may not take you to the Tower again."

He pulled the phaeton to a halt up on Tower Hill, facing the river. London Bridge spanned the murky waters just to the west, and the Tower of London sprawled below them, its bastions and stretches of wall wrapped around the core of the citadel, the White Tower.

"I wish," Nell said longingly, "I might just peek into the White Tower and the chapel."

"Not this time." Dev took up the reins and set the horses in motion. "It'll take hours, and no doubt Wicken is in a stew already, wondering what has become of you."

Dev proved himself immune to pleading and cajolery, but turned and proceeded at a fast clip toward Mayfair and St. James's.

When he pulled up in Chandos Street, Nell held out her hand. "Thank you, Dev," she said, looking up at him with a twinkle in her eyes. "Your manner of asking a lady to drive with you may be unorthodox, but I did enjoy it."

"I shall remember that."

She cocked her head, frowning a little. "It was the drive I enjoyed, mind you."

He laughed and sprang to the ground. Clasping Nell firmly around the middle, he swung her off the high perch. He did not let go of her immediately; instead, he tightened his grip.

"What a tiny waist. My hands can circle it, and with room to spare."

"What large hands you must have," Nell retorted, trying to sound unconcerned. His touch, even though he wore driving gloves, could not but recall the feel of his hand on her breast and the tingling flame it had ignited when he believed her to be Josephine. Even now, the warmth of a blush, starting at her midriff, spread slowly to her face.

"My lord, if you are as concerned about my reputation as you make out to be, surely you should unhand me now?"

Instantly he let go and stepped back, a mocking smile

twisting his shapely mouth. "None but you can guard your reputation, Nell, and the surest way is to give up that crazy notion of yours. Forget the academy. Find yourself a husband and raise a parcel of little brats if you're bored."

"What?!" she exclaimed. "You wish for more brats on your doorstep?"

"You and your brood will be in the country, for I still intend to buy your house."

She turned to mount the stairs to her front door. From the corner of her eye, she saw him run up the twin flight of marble steps leading to his door while his tiger drove the phaeton to the mews. Dev stood not three paces from her as she pressed down the handle, and his voice, low though it was, drifted clearly across the wrought-iron rail.

"I always get what I want. Remember that when you tend your cottage garden."

"Think of the mess boy in Spain, Devil Mackenzie. Then tell me who gets *her* way when her mind is made up." Nell whisked inside, slamming the door before he could utter a reply.

It was just as well she did not hear the string of oaths he muttered, Dev reflected wryly when he was capable of rational thought. In all likelihood she would have thrown them back in his face at the next opportunity.

Still feeling very much on edge, he changed into evening clothes and took himself off to his club, determined to put Number Two-A, Chandos Street and its pesky occupant from his mind. Alas for his intentions. No sooner had he settled himself in a quiet corner of one of the reading rooms, with a bottle of finest smuggled cognac for company, than the chamber was invaded by a dozen or so young officers on leave from the Peninsula.

They were an irrepressible bunch, and no matter how many frowns or outright reprimands from the older club members they drew upon themselves, they burst into boisterous speech again and again. Dev could not help but hear Nell's name, nor could he ignore the reading aloud of an advertisement in the *Morning Post*, recommending Miss Nell's Select Academy for Young Brides of His Majesty's Officers to those ladies wishing an introduction to the rigors of army life in India and the Peninsula.

To Dev's way of thinking, the officers—a great many of whom he had served with before selling out shortly after the deaths of his father and brother in the fall of '09—regarded Nell's enterprise in an entirely too frivolous manner.

"Pluck to the backbone, our Nell!" shouted Ensign Fairfield, who had been but a drummer boy when Dev knew him in Spain. "Damme, but I'm looking forward to seeing Nell. I'll call on her first thing in the morning."

"Why wait till morning?" Lieutenant Anthony Marple rapped a coin against his glass to gain attention. "I have a box at the Theatre Royal. Remember how Nell used to talk about wanting to see a play in London?"

"And we'll take the child to the Piazza for supper," said a major whose burnt face suggested a long stay in a climate even hotter than that of Spain's.

Dev's brittle temper snapped. His chair crashed into the wall as he jumped up and strode purposefully into their midst. "Are you mad?"

Ignoring cheerful greetings, he demanded, "Don't you see that you will ruin her? If you plan to call on her, at least do it during the day and have the sense to talk her out of this madness."

"Ho!" A newcomer, a captain in a blue hussar uniform, had entered and stood behind Dev. "Words of caution from Devil Mackenzie. I never thought to see the day."

"Cyprian!" Dev whirled, a wide grin curving his mouth. "What the devil—" He broke off, his smile replaced by a look of dismay when he saw Cyprian Westcott's right arm reposing in a sling of tooled leather. "Well," he said softly, "I need not ask what you're doing in England, my friend. How did it happen?"

"Skirmishing around Almeida." An expression of disgust twisted the captain's drawn features. "Just my luck to stand in the path of a stray bullet. And Wellington planning to take Fuentes de Oñoro! They may be fighting there even now."

"That's where Masséna is holed up." Dev's brows drew together in concern, but he could say no more. Cyprian was surrounded by officers and civilians alike, all clamoring for the latest news from the Peninsula. Dev listened quietly, but kept a wary eye on his friend, and when he noticed a thin film of perspiration on Cyprian's brow, he led him off to his own table.

"Have a drink, Cyprian. You look as queer as Dick's hatband."

"Damn, how I hate this waiting!" Closing his eyes, Cyprian tossed down a healthy measure of cognac. "Everyone asking me for news when I'm waiting for news myself. Takes longer for the curst dispatches to reach England than it takes us to fight a battle."

He held out his glass for a refill. "Almost as good as the stuff the French officers pass across the lines during nightwatch. Now what's all this about our sweet Nell?"

Dev raised a brow. " 'Sweet Nell'? More than just your arm must have been hit," he commented dryly. "The pesky brat's as prickly as ever."

"Never prickly with me, but then I've known her three months longer than you. Guess she has a soft spot for me."

"No need to boast about it," Dev said crossly.

"Why, what's this?" Raking his fingers through his dark hair, Cyprian directed a quizzing look at his friend. "Sounds as though your nose has been put out of joint. Don't tell me you've been caught at last and got the comeuppance you deserve."

Dev choked on his brandy. "Knew you for a romantic fool when you sent roses to that black-eyed barque of frailty in Lisbon," he said when at last he could speak again. "Believe me, old fellow, the woman who'll catch me in her toils has not been born."

"Then why does the mere mention of Nell make you fly into a pelter?"

"Nell not only spoiled the most delightful set-up I had with a very obliging lady, she also plans to start some infernal academy for brides right next door to me."

"I read the advertisement."

"I've offered to buy her half of the house. My greataunt Augusta's, you may remember. But Nell refuses to sell."

Cyprian tried in vain to suppress a smirk. "So, Miss Nell has elected to cross swords with you, has she?"

"With the buttons off."

"Lud, what I wouldn't give to be able to watch the two of you."

A sudden grin lit Dev's features. "Stay with me while you're in town."

"Done." Cyprian extended his left hand. "Bet you a monkey that Nell's academy will be firmly established—say, the end of the month."

Dev was not one to lightly refuse a wager, and the challenging gleam in Cyprian's eyes put him on his mettle.

"Done," he said, clasping the proffered hand. "I give you twenty-to-one that I'll take the house from her before the end of the month."

Chapter Five

It was not until the wee hours of the morning that the two gentlemen ascended with unsteady legs the stairs of Number Two, Chandos Street.

"Devil a bit!" Panting, Cyprian clung to the newel post on the second floor landing. "Bedroom's always on the top floor. Stupid arrangement, if you ask me."

Taking care not to jar Cyprian's injured arm, Dev helped him up the last flight. "Damn stubborn fool," he muttered. "Drunk as a brewer's horse, and feverish to boot."

"What 'bout you? Trying to gammon me you're shob —sober as a judge?"

"A trifle disguised, mayhap," Dev admitted, concentrating all the while on keeping a straight line toward the guest chamber. "But, then, brandy can do me no harm. *I* haven't been cupped by my physician."

"Put leeches on me, the old bloodsucker." Cyprian collapsed on the bed. He was shivering, and his eyes held a glassy look.

Dev covered him with a quilt, wishing it were he resting his head against the downy pillows. *A pox on all women, and particularly on that tawny-haired brat next door. Can't even forget about her at my club.*

He gave the bell cord above the bed a vicious tug, summoning his valet.

"Masterton," Dev enunciated carefully when that worthy appeared in the doorway, "look after Captain Westcott. I shall put myself to bed."

"Very well, my lord." The lanky, middle-aged gentleman's gentleman ran an expert eye over the recumbent form on the bed. "The captain shouldn't have indulged, if I may say so."

"Say anything you wish, only make him comfortable."

"That I will, my lord." Masterton nodded gloomily. "But I shouldn't wonder if he'll shoot the cat afore long."

"Give him some of that noxious brew you serve me when I'm bosky."

Dev hastily left the room before Masterton could take it into his head that he, too, stood in need of the infamous posset. Speed, however, was something his body resented. The woven runner laid out in the corridor rose toward him like a snake charmed by a fakir's pipe. The stairwell danced to the left, then back to the right. And when he tried to steady himself against the wall, it receded from his outstretched hand.

Groaning, Dev closed his eyes, but that set his head reeling. He fixed his gaze on his bedroom door, then charged ahead, past the fickle stairs into his chamber where he threw himself onto the four-poster bed that seemed to fill the whole room with its vastness.

After a while, he was able to sit up and remove his coat and shoes. Sinking back against the pillows, he tugged at his cravat until it came loose and flung it to the floor. After he opened his shirt to the waist, he was aware of momentary relief, of gritty, burning eyelids pressing down and relaxing, of a faint call, "Four o'clock and all's well," just before oblivion claimed him.

* * *

An explosion buffeted his head. His eyes flew open—and closed instantly against a blinding glare. It took him a moment to realize that he was in his own chamber and not on the battlefield of Coruña; that the piercing light was not caused by shells bursting around him, but was merely a strip of morning sun invading his window. Some blundering fool had neglected to draw the curtains.

Dev heaved himself upright. He groaned, clenching his teeth as his stomach rose with him. Vicious gnomes chiseled and hammered away behind his temples. No doubt that was what had made him dream of a detonation.

He had just dropped back against the pillows when a second explosion jerked his head up. A pistol shot. Very close by.

Perspiration drenched his skin. *Not again! It couldn't be happening twice.*

Dev rolled out of bed, his hands pressed to his pounding head. He snatched his own pistol from a dresser drawer, cocked it, and stumbled out into the hallway.

"Robbers! Thieves!" Masterton darted from the guest chamber like a fox who had caught the scent of hounds. "We'll all be murdered, my lord!"

"Stow your jabber, man," Dev commanded. "Did it come from downstairs?"

"No, my lord. Right here. I swear I thought you was bein' murdered in your own bed."

"Stuff and nonsense." Dev cocked his head, listening for further sounds that might give away the position of the intruder.

A third shot made him whirl around. He broke into a cold sweat. The report had come from behind the dividing wall. *Nell! Someone was attacking Nell!*

Dev sprinted down the stairs, four at a time, slipped in his stockinged feet, and smashed his already splitting head against the baluster. He caught himself, rushed on down and out his front door, landing with one foot in a mop bucket.

With a curse and a kick he sent it tumbling down the marble steps. The scullery maid, her eyes round with terror, jabbed her brush toward Nell's door.

It stood ajar.

It seemed to Dev that he couldn't move, that fear of what he might find inside held him tied to the spot, but already he had vaulted the iron rail dividing the stoop, already he forged up the narrow stairs to Nell's bedroom.

A fourth shot sent him hurtling up the last steps. One part of his mind registered that the shooting originated down the hall, not in Nell's bedchamber; the other part started nagging at him about the number of shots and the intervals at which they were fired.

As he turned into the corridor, he saw the open doorway of the last apartment on his left. Without a check he burst inside—and stopped.

Nell, with her side to him, was facing a target range. She was alive. Unhurt.

Mopping his damp brow with a shirt sleeve, he exhaled in a gusty sigh. But relief was only temporary. Other, more primitive emotions surged in his breast.

"I'll be damned," he muttered hoarsely.

"Hush, Wicken! Watch this," Nell said without taking her eyes off the targets. The small, silver-mounted pistol she had pointed at Dev during his ill-fated sojourn in her bedroom nestled in her right hand, aimed straight at a tiger's head.

She pulled the trigger. The report echoed in the small room; a plume of acrid smoke wafted to the ceiling, then dissipated.

"Dead center!" Nell clapped her hands and did a little skip of excitement. "Five shots, and—" She broke off, her eyes widening when Dev appeared in her line of sight. "Oh," she said. "It's you."

"Five shots. Congratulations, Nell. You killed the tiger."

Something in his tone alerted her to danger. At a glance, she took in the pistol in his hand, his tousled hair, his open shirt escaping from the waistband of his pantaloons, and his stockinged feet, one of them leaving wet imprints on the floorboards as he strode toward her.

"I woke you up. I am sorry, Dev." Prudently, Nell retreated to a small chest of drawers under the windows upon which was set a piece of flannel, a powder flask, bullets, and cartridge papers. Her gaze lingered on the already prepared cartridges. It would take no time at all to reload. . . .

Resolutely, she set down her pistol. "Did you go down heavy at the card table? Or was it Blue Ruin that made you sleep so late?"

"Late!" His voice rose to a roar, and he covered the short space between them in a leap. "It's the middle of the night. And you have the impudence, the infernal—"

"Gall?" she supplied with a quizzing look when he groaned and pressed a fist to his forehead. She noticed how pale he was under his tan and how unsteady his hand was.

Her voice had a reviving effect, however. He tossed his pistol next to hers. His hands went around her neck. Fury as hot as an Indian funeral pyre blazed from his eyes.

"How easy it would be to strangle you. Didn't I warn you, brat? But strangling would be a reward compared to the punishment you deserve."

Nell did not waste her breath on speech. She raised a foot and brought it down sharply on his instep, then kicked his shin for good measure—gaining five very sore toes in the process. Recouping, she balled her fists, aiming at Dev's nose. He was faster. Gripping her elbows, he pinned her arms to her sides.

"You may kick as much as you like," he said with a laugh that made her shiver. "But you shan't strike me."

Her own temper rose. "How generous. You know very well I cannot kick you with slippers."

"You should have thought of that before you set out to annoy me."

"I did not! I had not planned to get up your dander." She tried to twist free, but only hurt the tender skin on her inner arms under his relentless grip.

"What is it with you?" she cried. "You come charging in here like some high priest of the Inquisition, accusing me of rousing you in the dead of night." She looked pointedly at the window where the bright glow of the May sun was clearly visible. "And not content with that, you must needs maul and threaten me. Why, you are nothing but a great big oaf! A bullyboy picking on someone half his size."

His hands dropped from her arms as though they had turned into red-hot coals under his touch. "I suspected you're unfit to live in civilized surroundings. That has been amply confirmed," he said scathingly. "In society, Miss Ignorant, the day does not begin until eleven, or later. And we do not shoot pistols in the confines of our homes, rousing our neighbors to nightmarish fears.''

Rubbing her arms, she glared at him defiantly. "I did not believe it possible that the shots could be heard outside the house.''

"Unhappily, we share this house.''

"Well, then, henceforth I shall not practice target shooting until *after* eleven of the clock.''

"You won't shoot at all. Why, if shooting and loading a pistol is what you plan to teach the unfortunate young brides, you'll turn half the officers into widowers before they've become accustomed to matrimony.''

Stung, Nell took a threatening step toward him. "You are insufferable,'' she choked out. "I hate you, Devil Mackenzie! If I were a man, I'd plant you a facer so that you wouldn't dare show yourself at your club for a fortnight.''

He glared back at her, but what he saw apparently tickled his funny bone, for he broke into a shout of laughter. "You look fit to burst, brat. Watch it, or you'll have an apoplexy before you're a day older.''

"Get out!''

Still laughing, he picked up his pistol, uncocked it, and stuck it in the waistband of his pantaloons. There was a swagger in his step as he walked to the door.

Nell fired a parting shot. "And a fine sight *you* are, Devil Mackenzie! Lost your valet, have you?''

She might have added more, but just as Dev reached the doorway and turned back to salute her with a mocking bow, Wicken pushed into the chamber.

"Miss Nell,'' he said severely. "Seems I can't leave ye for a moment without ye misbehavin'. I could hear ye the minute I came up the front steps. And the lady hammering on the door as though she was wishful of drivin' the knocker straight through the wood.''

"What lady?'' Nell forgot about Dev and her anger at him. "Tell me, Wicken. Might she be my first pupil?''

Wicken shook his head. "Not she,'' he said with conviction. He darted a sidelong look from Dev to Nell, noting her moue of disappointment. "But mayhap the young girl with her would fit the bill.''

Nell's face lit up. "Where have you put them? Oh, dear! Do I look dignified? Is my gown severe enough?"

Wicken frowned repressively. "Good thing I put 'em in the small parlor on the ground floor. If the older lady heard ye carryin' on, Miss Nell, she'd have her daughter out of here in a pig's whisper. And what about the lieutenant—the marquis, I should say?"

"Oh." Nell threw a disinterested glance at Dev, who had unashamedly listened to the exchange. "He does look disreputable, doesn't he? Just what I've been telling him. Perhaps he had better stay up here until the ladies have left."

Dev's expression was unreadable. Not a muscle twitched in his face as he returned her look. "As you wish," he said with disquieting meekness.

That, and a certain gleam in his eyes, aroused instant suspicion in her breast. Dev was not a man to be ordered around with impunity, but she could not afford to waste time placating him. She hurried off, and when she faced her visitors in the narrow room overlooking Chandos Street, all thought of Dev was wiped from her mind.

Mrs. Margood, a stern-faced widow in her fifties, came straight to the point after the briefest of introductions had been performed. "Miss Hetherington," she said in clipped, well-modulated accents, "I fear there has been a misunderstanding."

"Oh?" Nell tried to look interested yet demure, but she could not help staring at the lady's thin nose and mouth, at the thin, straight back that refused to lean against the cushions of the Queen Anne settle.

"On *my* part, no doubt," Mrs. Margood added with a smile as thin as her nose. "You see, I expected a lady of mature years, an officer's widow, perhaps, to teach my child how to go on in India. You appear to be younger than my daughter, and you're unmarried. Hardly qualified to teach her."

The daughter, seventeen or eighteen, Nell judged, blushed and hung her head. Poor little mouse. She'd be one of those clinging, wilting wives who drove their doting husbands insane with fears and alarums—unless she understood exactly what to expect.

Nell shifted in her chair and met Mrs. Margood's cold

eyes. "It is not my intent to instruct young ladies in their wifely duties. I should think a mother would consider it her prerogative to do so."

"Miss Hetherington!" The older woman bristled in outrage.

"Indeed, ma'am, if you read my advertisement, you must be aware that I plan to provide my pupils with knowledge of the lifestyle they may expect, preparing them for a different climate and inherent hazards, and giving them tools to ensure a certain amount of comfort in India or the Peninsula."

"And what might be your qualifications?"

"I was raised following the drum, Mrs. Margood. My father was Major Jack Hetherington. My mother traveled everywhere with him. I was born in Mysore, lived at various times in Punjab, Bengal, Burma, and Ceylon, and in 1808 removed with my parents to the Peninsula. Does that meet with your requirements?"

The lady seemed at a loss. "Well—I daresay . . ."

"Oh, pray, Mama!" Miss Margood swallowed nervously. Two bright spots of color graced her pale cheeks. "I should like to take instructions from Miss Hetherington," she blurted out.

"Upon my word!" blustered her mama. "I hardly know what to say."

At that moment, the parlor door swung open. On the threshold, in the full glory of his disheveled maleness, stood the Marquis of Ellsworth. He seemed to see only Nell. There was a fire in his eyes, and the smile he directed at her contained the promise of seduction.

"Nell, my love," he said, his deep voice making every word a caress, "you promised not to be gone above a minute."

A cannonball could not have had a more devastating effect. Mrs. Margood shot straight up from her seat, her eyes bulging and her face taking on a purplish red hue. Her mouth opened and closed several times, but not a sound issued forth.

Miss Margood, after casting a timid glance at her mama, blushed a rosy red, then hung her head to peep at the handsome, half-clad gentleman from beneath her lowered lashes.

And Nell? She sat in dawning horror, her eyes riveted to the pistol in his waistband and the expanse of tanned skin and chestnut hair exposed by his open shirt—like some common pirate! Her mind refused to believe what she had heard. *Surely he would not . . . could not . . . !*

The gleam in his eyes became more pronounced. She recognized it now. It was the same glint that had disturbed her when he had, oh, so meekly, agreed to remain upstairs. He had planned this all along. Her punishment. His retribution.

Horror gave way to calm. She knew just what she must do. Slowly she rose. Forcing herself to smile, she walked toward him.

"Oh, you naughty boy," she chided softly. "Are you hiding from Wicken again?"

She turned to the still speechless Mrs. Margood. "My brother," she said in a stage whisper. "You must excuse the poor dear. After Coruña he has never been himself again. Caught a piece of shot in his head, you know."

A choking sound from Dev alarmed her, but Mrs. Margood had regained control over her tongue and started to speak in an outraged voice, covering any further sounds from the "afflicted brother."

"Upon my word, Miss Hetherington! These are strange goings-on. I don't know that I'd care to leave my daughter in a house with a madman."

"He doesn't get away from his keeper more than once a year. Miss Margood will be quite safe, I assure you." Not daring to meet Dev's eyes, Nell said briskly, "Come along now. You've—"

"Oh, the poor, dear man!" Miss Margood exclaimed suddenly. "Oh, look, Mama. He's crying!"

Nell looked up quickly. And, indeed, she saw tears roll down his cheeks. She also noted, however, the tightly closed eyes, the twitching mouth, and his suspiciously doubled-over stance. He was laughing, the devil.

Desperation lending her additional strength, Nell pushed him out the door.

"Wicken!" she shouted just as someone rapped the knocker against the brass plate on the front door. Instead of waiting patiently to be admitted, the newcomer tried the handle and, finding the door unlocked, blithely stepped inside.

"Nell, my darlin' girl," said Captain Cyprian Westcott,

very well pleased at not having to go look for her. "What a scare you gave us. Masterton, Dev's valet, y'know, would have it that you'd been murdered like Dev's—"

"Cyprian!" Nell abandoned Dev to Mrs. Margood and cast herself on Captain Westcott's broad chest to be caught in a fierce, one-armed hug.

"How absolutely marvelous to see you. But your arm —are you all right?" Anxiously she searched his face, noting the dark shadows under his eyes, the sunken cheeks.

"Never better. The sawbones assured me I'd have no more than a four-week leave. But let me look at you, my darlin'." He held her at arm's length to study her at leisure.

His gray-green eyes widened with that same warm look she had seen him cast at some of the younger ladies in Lisbon. "Grown up at last," he said softly. "I think you had better give me another kiss."

"Well! Upon my word!" Mrs. Margood's thin chest swelled with indignation. Snatching her daughter's hand, she dragged the girl toward the front door.

"Stand aside, sir." Head held high, she sailed past Cyprian, who had courteously opened the door for her. Her voice, a little too high and too shrill for a well-bred lady, was clearly audible from the street.

"A house of ill-repute. Well, I never! We must stop at Lansdowne House. We'll see what the dowager countess has to say about *this*."

Nell whirled and turned her rekindling wrath on Dev, who had sunk onto the second-to-last stair. With his head on his knees and both hands pressed to his temples, he was a sight of pure misery. Except that his shoulders shook.

"You abominable, insufferable fiend! I'll never forgive you for this. Never!"

Dev raised bloodshot eyes to her. "Dammit, Nell," he said with a groan. "Must you shout? My head's pounding like an artillery gun."

"And no more than you deserve."

"I say, Nell." Cyprian lowered himself carefully onto the step beside Dev. "You're in a puckish temper today. What has the poor fellow done except fly *ventre à terre* to your rescue? By the way, what happened to the would-be murderer? Did you slay him, Dev?"

"It was all a hum. Nell was indulging in a bit of target practice."

Cyprian's face lit up with unholy glee. "And you rushed off hotfoot! On that tidbit I can dine out for weeks."

"Not if you wish to retain the services of your good arm, you won't."

Nell glared at Dev. "Why, you brute!"

"Don't be a widgeon, Nell," Cyprian said hastily. "He's only bamming. Besides, I shouldn't tease him about his gallantry. Would have come myself, except that fool Masterton had taken away my uniform to be pressed. Wouldn't have wished to have me appear in a nightshirt, would you?"

"No," said Nell, a reluctant smile tugging at the corners of her mouth. "That would really have put the fat in the fire."

"Unfair, Nell." Dev looked at her reproachfully. "Why are you cross-as-crabs with me and not with him? After calling me a naughty boy, too, when it was *his* demanding another kiss that put the beldame to flight. She was very willing to accept me as your dicked-in-the-nob brother."

"Cyprian has an injured arm."

"And my head hurts."

"Mayhap you *are* queer in the attic," Nell suggested sweetly.

Dev rose. "Come, Cyprian," he said, holding out his hand to help his friend up. "I can take a hint that I'm not wanted. Let's give Nell a chance to come off her high ropes."

"Take a damper. She doesn't want *me* to go," Cyprian pointed out, but, responding to his friend's dark frown, he rose and followed as Dev, without a glance at Nell, made his dignified way out.

When the two gentlemen were comfortably ensconced in Dev's study, a tray filled with slices of bread and cold meats between them and tumblers of foaming porter in their hands, Cyprian said, "And why the devil did you not want me to stay next door? Think I'll cut you out?"

Dev cast him a look of irritation. "Don't be daft, Cyprian. For one thing, she lives alone. No chaperon save for Wicken."

"Jack's batman. Why, he's more protective of her than

the most ferocious lady companion could be. Heard he lost an arm, though.''

''I have no fear that he can protect her, one arm or two. Thing is, he's not acceptable as a chaperon. Ladies of the *ton* will tear Nell to shreds if word gets about that she receives gentlemen callers without some other lady lending her countenance.''

Cyprian watched his friend speculatively. ''Damn unusual for Devil Mackenzie to worry about the proprieties, isn't it?''

Dev took a large swallow of his porter. ''Hell,'' he said finally. ''She's Jack's brat. What would you have me do?''

''There's that,'' Cyprian said solemnly, then, veering off on another tack, ''Come to White's with me for a rubber of whist?''

''I shall have a bath and a shave. Must also write a note to Lady Lansdowne. Nell said she knew her in India.''

Dev stood up, stretched, and indulged in a wide yawn. ''Don't gamble away all your pay in one session. I'm planning to take your money myself in a nice little game of piquet.''

On these words, he hauled himself up to his room, pulling off his shirt on the way. He removed the pistol from his waistband and was about to place it in the top dresser-drawer when he caught sight of a large key at the back.

His eyes lit up with a mischievous gleam, and a devilish grin tugged at the corners of his mouth as he set the pistol down beside the key and pushed the drawer shut.

By George! If it hadn't slipped his mind that he had *two* keys to the cellars of Number Two-A.

Chapter Six

Nell remained in the vestibule after the front door had closed behind Cyprian and Dev. First the hapless door and then the dividing wall received a look heavy with anger, defiance, and, finally, resolution.

So Dev was set on plaguing her until she'd give up the house, was he? *But it won't fadge, my lord. You must have windmills in your head if you believe I'm that easily routed.*

Nell's forehead smoothed, and her eyes took on a far-away look as she composed scheme after delightful scheme to show the Marquis of Ellsworth her mettle.

She dismissed the notion of leaving orders with Wicken that she was not at home when Dev called. It was unworthy of her. She would receive Dev and make him regret his interference. She would prove that she could stand her ground in London just as well as she could in the wilds of India and the Peninsula.

But first she'd get Cyprian on her side.

"Wicken!" she called, wondering why he had not responded to her earlier summons when she needed his help removing Dev from Mrs. Margood's presence.

She had just set foot on the stairs to search for Wicken on the second floor or in the target room when she heard his heavy tread approach from the nether regions.

"Couldn't find any black pepper," he said, coming into view. "So I just popped out to fetch us some."

He carried a large tumbler, and as he stepped closer, Nell caught a whiff of something that strongly brought the late Jack Hetherington to mind.

Her nose wrinkled. "What on earth are you drinking, Wicken?"

"Not me, Miss Nell. It's for the lieutenant. A mighty sore head is what he earned himself last night, and Major Jack always said as this was the only cure."

"Papa's pepper-posset!" said Nell, outraged. "Wicken, I absolutely forbid you to pander to the marquis's comfort. If he cannot hold his liquor, he shouldn't get bosky."

"Now, Miss Nell—"

"Besides, he's gone."

With a look of resignation, Wicken set the tumbler on the hall table. "About supper, Miss Nell. The butcher boy delivered a nice leg o' lamb, and this mornin', while I was fetchin' the paper, I also got us some beans an' some fresh mint. D'ye want me to—"

"I'll cook supper," Nell said loftily. "You have enough to do clearing out the cellars and the attic. But first—" Distractedly she tapped a slippered foot. "Wicken, is there a recipe book in the kitchen?"

"Whatever for? Ye never needed none to roast a leg o' lamb in Portugal."

"I thought I'd bake some of those little cakes the Marquesa de Jaraiz sent Papa when we were camped near Salamanca. Captain Westcott is staying with the marquis. I plan to invite him to tea."

"The captain!" Wicken's face lit up, then crumpled in concern. "Only one reason that the captain would come home. Got himself shot to bits, didn't he?"

"He assured me it's a mere scratch, but"—Nell frowned—"that's what you said about *your* arm when we were evacuated from Coruña."

"Don't ye worrit none, Miss Nell. They tell me the surgeons have learned a bit since then. For one thing, they're not as quick and ready ter amputate as they was when *my* arm started festerin'."

She gave him a quick, grateful smile. "I'll give you a note for Captain Westcott. Please deliver it straight away."

When Wicken had departed with the invitation, Nell

descended to the kitchen to wage a war with butter, sugar, flour, vanilla, and, more deadly, with the ancient wood-burning stove.

Two hours later, after she had entrusted her third offering to the cavernous recess of the oven, Wicken appeared in the large basement room with its tiled walls and floor. He pushed her bodily into a chair at the cluttered kitchen table, whisked away a dozen dirty bowls, the charred remains of Nell's previous baking efforts, and set before her a glass of wine.

"Now drink up like a good girl," he ordered. "An' have a morsel of this chicken I fetched from me sister's chop house. She's a fair cook, is me sister Meg, if I say so meself."

"And I meant to prepare luncheon as well as dinner." Guiltily Nell surveyed the havoc she had wreaked, then glanced down at her flour-dusted gown. "I must change soon unless I want Captain Westcott to mistake me for a miller's daughter."

"There's plenty of time. The captain was out when I took yer note. Gone to White's. He'll not be back until four or five, the butler told me."

"And the marquis?" Nell asked with studied indifference.

"Ah, well. The marquis, he was at home, but since yer invitation didn't include him—"

"Never mind, Wicken. I'm sure I don't care if I *never* see him again."

Wicken looked doubtful, but he only said, "If ye would consider takin' a peep at the clock now and again, Miss Nell, ye might succeed with one or t'other of the next batches of cake."

"Oh!" Dropping the chicken wing she had been nibbling onto her plate, Nell flew to the oven. She was about to fling the heavy door open when Wicken thrust a towel into her hand.

"Nice an' easy, Miss Nell. If ye let too much draft in all at once, the cake will fall. I learned *that* much while I was stayin' with me sister. And never touch the oven door without wrappin' yer hand."

Obediently, she wound the towel around her palm and fingers, then slowly lowered the door. A delicious aroma wafted from the hot interior.

"By Jupiter," she said reverently. "I did it. It's not burnt, Wicken!"

He narrowed his eyes at the flat, pale brown cake. He'd eat his empty sleeve if Miss Nell hadn't forgotten the eggs. But he couldn't tell her. She'd start all over and probably make matters worse. Besides, she was as proud as a peacock of her labors.

"If ye want them Frenchified cakes," he said, "them petty furs, best cut 'em while hot. An' drown 'em with icing," he advised, then stamped off to answer the summons of the door knocker.

Nell had just completed cutting the diamond-shaped little cakes when he returned. "The Dowager Countess of Lansdowne," he announced.

"Botheration!" Nell's hands flew to her hair, then brushed ineffectually at the floury skirt of her gown. "How did she find out I'm here? Well, the countess has never been one to stand on ceremony. She'll take me as I am, I suppose, for I shan't change until I've finished the icing. I must have pink icing. How do I get pink, Wicken?"

"Try cherry juice," he muttered, his arm elbow-deep in sudsy water as he started to rinse the evidence of Nell's housewifely efforts.

"Thank you, Wicken. For everything." Nell blew him a kiss before gathering her skirts and rushing up the stairs. There was no one in the downstairs parlor, so she hurried on to the next floor.

Smiling, she stepped into the drawing room. "Lady Lansdowne! How wonderful to see you again."

The white-haired lady, who had been engaged in a thorough inspection of chairs and tables with the aid of a gold-handled lorgnette, swung her bulk around.

"Dust," the dowager countess said reprovingly. "I cannot abide dust. And Augusta's chairs. Tsk! The covers are in dire need of—" The lorgnette pointed at Nell. "My dear child, you look absolutely dreadful."

"Don't I, though?" Laughing, and feeling again like the fourteen-year-old who had been indiscriminately doled scolds and sugarplums, Nell embraced the gruff old lady. "And you look absolutely stunning."

"Fustian!" Trying to conceal her pleasure, the countess

patted her crimped locks beneath a purple velvet turban before lowering herself carefully onto one of the despised chairs. "I can't abide humbuggers, Nell. I'll never see eighty again, and that's the melancholy truth. My doctor, the old fool, tells me I'm too fat, but I'll outlive him yet. See if I don't!"

"Of course you will," Nell said warmly. "Let me get you a cup of tea, ma'am, and then we may enjoy a comfortable coze."

Behind the lorgnette, the dark eyes narrowed with amusement. As a child, Nell had always thought they resembled currants stuck in a pudding, and she found that even now she was not above making such a comparison.

"A coze!" A deep, rich chuckle shook Lady Lansdowne's ample bosom. "You know I don't waste my time on foolishness. Only thing I enjoy is gossip. Now sit down, gal. I don't have time for tea." More softly, she added, "First, let me tell you how sorry I was to hear of the death of your dear parents."

"Thank you."

"I wrote to you when the casualty lists of Coruña were published in *The Times*. Left the letter at the Admiralty, but after six months they returned it. Said they didn't know what had become of you, only that you had come to England on one of the transports."

"I went to Bath. Taught at Miss Mofty's Select Academy."

Lady Lansdowne raised her brows. "Your mama must have educated you better than I thought if you were qualified for a teaching position."

"I taught languages."

"Ah, yes. I remember now. You were like a parrot. If you heard a phrase once, it stayed with you." Again her rumbling chuckle set her bulk in motion. "More often than not it got you into trouble when you repeated something quite unsuitable for a young lady."

"I never pretended to be a lady."

"You *are* a lady. Don't you forget it, gal! And that brings me to the purpose of my visit, for it appears," the countess said severely, "that for once the young scamp, Stanford's heir—what's his name?"

"Devil Mackenzie," Nell said with foreboding.

"Hey-ho! Devil! Wonderfully suitable, of course, but I'm speaking of Ellsworth."

"One and the same, ma'am. Devil Mackenzie is what his friends called him in the Peninsula."

"Ah, yes. Forgot that he's a Mackenzie on his mother's side. And, of course, they're all devils, those Highland men. Handsome devils."

"Has he been carrying tales about me?" Nell demanded.

"Wrote me a perfectly civil note this morning. Let me know that you moved into Augusta Fawnhope's house, and why the dickens you haven't come to see me is more than I can understand. I'm quite out of charity with you, gal."

"But I only moved in on the second! Three days ago. And Dev only told me yesterday that you're my neighbor. I planned to call, I assure you." . . . *and prevent Dev from setting you against me.*

The current eyes narrowed until they all but disappeared in the mounds of flesh that were Lady Lansdowne's lids and cheeks. "And *how* were you planning to make your calls since you've nary a coach, an abigail, or a companion to lend you consequence?"

"The wretch! I'll teach him to interfere in my life."

Lady Lansdowne had no trouble recognizing the Marquis of Ellsworth as the wretch. "He's right, gal. You cannot live alone in London. Not unless you want the *ton* to think you're thumbing your nose at them. I already had Mrs. Margood descend on me and raise a fuss about you. Something about you running a house of ill-repute on my doorstep?"

A questioning look at Nell elicited only a hastily stifled giggle. "Well," said the dowager comfortably, "I soon sent her about her business. Never fear that she'll come poking her thin nose into your affairs again, but is there no one you could ask to live with you? Some impoverished relative? A friend?"

"I've written to Bess Wainwright, the widow of one of Papa's friends. The marquis," Nell added impulsively, "calls her a silly widgeon."

The countess dismissed Dev's words with a wave of her pudgy hand. "Bess was a Farnham before her marriage. One of the Kent Farnhams. She's rather young, but that connection will do you no harm." Nodding her beturbaned and beplumed head with satisfaction, she decreed, "She must move in immediately. And now, gal, you had best tell me all about this school you're planning to open."

"It seems you already know everything," Nell said indignantly.

"Don't get on your high ropes with me, young lady. What I've learned is nothing to the point. I want to hear it from you."

The dowager countess listened, stern and unsmiling at first, but slowly she relaxed, and when Nell had finished outlining her plans, Lady Lansdowne's face was wreathed in smiles.

"You'll do, gal," she said gruffly. "But then I'm not surprised. Always thought you were as sharp as a pin."

With Nell's help, Lady Lansdowne heaved her bulk off the dainty chair and down the stairs to the vestibule.

"Tell that fool man of yours"—the old lady puffed, breathless—"to show me into a ground-floor room next time I come calling."

Nell opened the front door for her guest. "He'll be disappointed, ma'am. On the ground floor I have only a shabby little parlor, hardly what Wicken would consider right for someone of your exalted station."

"Hardly less shabby than the drawing room," the countess retorted as she accepted the strong arms of her two footmen, who had been waiting patiently on the stoop.

They deposited the old lady tenderly in her carriage, an elegant affair drawn by four magnificent black horses, then, with perfect timing, swung themselves onto their perches at the rear just as the coach began to roll.

A smile played about Nell's mouth when she returned to the kitchen, and a lightness of spirits remained with her while she iced the *petits fours*, then retired to her room to change. Not until Lady Lansdowne had given her tacit approval of Miss Nell's Select Academy, had she acknowledged her own fears of failing in her venture.

Her savings were minimal—one-hundred-odd pounds her father had placed in her care just before Soult's attack at Coruña, and eighty pounds saved during her three years at Miss Mofty's. She had received no encouragement in her endeavors until the dowager countess had smiled in acceptance. Miss Mofty had been doubtful; Mr. Forsythe and Wicken clearly disapproving; and Dev, besides showing his contempt for her plans, had left her in no doubt that he would oppose her in any way he could.

"Pshaw," muttered Nell as she pulled a gown of deep blue sarcenet over her head. "I thrive on opposition."

She pirouetted on high-heeled slippers, delighting in the way the gown fluttered around her ankles. It was cut in the high-waisted fashion, but unlike taller ladies, Nell disdained the use of a sash or a riband below her breasts. Nor had she hemmed the gown with layers of flounces, which would only make her appear shorter. Instead, to give the skirt some heaviness, she had faced it with gold trim from India.

All in all, she was satisfied with her appearance as she hurried down the stairs to the drawing room where the tea service was set out and everything—save for the kettle of boiling water Wicken would bring up later—was in readiness for her visitor. It was well past four o'clock. Surely Cyprian would have returned from White's by now.

At the sound of a firm tread on the stairs, Nell turned to the open drawing room door with a smile on her face. The footsteps halted. A shock of chestnut hair, brushed into the artful disarray of the "windswept," appeared around the doorjamb. A pair of blue eyes laughed at her.

"Is it safe to enter? Wouldn't want you to mistake my head for that of a tiger." Dev sauntered into the drawing room, so blatantly certain of a welcome that he instantly set up her hackles.

She gave him a look of pure loathing. "Where is Cyprian?"

"At White's, I believe. Playing whist. Aren't you going to ask me to sit down?"

"And you came to make his excuses? How kind of you. Well, I don't plan to keep you standing long, my lord. What I have to say to *you* won't take above a minute. Then you may leave."

"Still in a pelter, I see."

He stepped close to her. So close that, despite her high heels, she had to tilt her head back to look at him. It was an experience that gave her ample cause to regret her impulsive refusal to offer him a chair.

"You chose to fight me," he said softly. "You must learn to become a good loser."

His nearness was disturbing, threatening. Nell took a step backwards. She felt a chair press against the back of her knees, and abruptly sat down. "Perhaps, my lord, you had better take a seat after all, and learn to be a good loser yourself."

"As you wish." There was amusement in his voice, but also, she thought, a certain amount of wariness. "What scheme are you hatching now?"

"I want to thank you for your exertions on my behalf."

"Always happy to oblige, of course. What exactly is it that I'm supposed to have done for you?"

"Lady Lansdowne paid me a visit. I must admit that I hadn't dared hope to gain her support, but due to your kind offices, my lord, she is quite in charity with me and my plans."

Nell watched him closely, but if he felt chagrin at the news, he did not show it. He stretched out his long legs, crossing them at the ankles, and flicked absently at a speck of imagined dust on his fawn-colored pantaloons.

"Excellent. Perhaps she can get you invited to some soiree or ball. That, my dear, is where you can catch yourself a husband," he said, regarding her from beneath lazily drooping lids. "Not with the best intent in the world could I have gotten you an introduction to the *ton*. Bachelors, you know, are looked upon askance as squires of innocent young maidens."

"Especially when they're known as squires of straw-damsels," Nell countered.

"Or if the young lady could be mistaken for one because she insists on living unchaperoned."

"I shall have Bess Wainwright living with me."

Dev smiled disarmingly. "Don't eat me, Nell. Now that everything is in the way of being settled for you, you should try to behave toward me in a more conciliatory manner. Lady Lansdowne may be able to smooth your path, but a few dances with the Marquis of Ellsworth, or a drive in the park, are not to be sneezed at. I can help you become the belle of the season."

"Why, you swell-head! I'd sooner be a wallflower than grovel at your feet."

He chuckled. "What a picture you draw. Forgive me, Nell. I had forgot how fiercely independent you are. Of course, you'll want to achieve your success without my negligible assistance. But," he said, turning serious, "a season in London requires funds, and there, I *can* help."

He was unperturbed by the flash of anger in her gray eyes. "You can rent a house, pay your companion, a cook, a maid, and still have enough of the ready to buy yourself a dozen ball gowns. And a dozen will not be enough if you're planning to cut a dash. I'm renewing my offer, Nell. Raise it by five thousand pounds."

Her anger dissipated as quickly as it had flared up. A mischievous smile flitted across her face. "How I do misjudge you. If I didn't think at first that you were offering to finance my season, giving me *carte blanche*, you know?"

He rose, his expression grim. "You thought nothing of the kind. You realized there's no alternative but to sell the house to me, and that went against the grain with you."

"I *don't* need to sell. I am not planning to have a season. Besides, I can sew my own gowns. I can even cook."

"Camp-fire cooking."

Nell snatched the plate of *petits fours* off the table and thrust it at him. "Here! Judge for yourself."

He recoiled, looking at the grayish pink diamonds with suspicion. "After you, madam."

"Craven!" Picking up one of the pieces, Nell bit into it with relish. Shock registered on her face, and the crunching sound when she chewed told its own tale.

Laughing, Dev walked to the door. "Mayhap you should send the recipe to the War Department. They're always looking for deadly missiles to fill into their shells. Ouch!"

He swung around, rubbing the back of his head where the hard little cake had hit him. "You . . . brat!"

Not trusting the look in his eyes as he strode toward her, Nell hurled the plate. Dev ducked, and Nell's only weapon broke into tiny shards as it hit the door frame.

Dev towered before her, tall and implacable. His fingers bit into her upper arms. She stood quite still, looking up at him and meeting his anger with defiance, although inwardly she quaked. He was so very furious, and so very large. But Nell Hetherington would always stand her ground.

"You," he said in menacing tones, "deserve to be spanked."

"You shouldn't have provoked me."

"And I," he continued, "would derive no mean pleasure from laying you across my knee and administering said spanking."

She tossed her head. "As though I didn't know it."

"Unfortunately, you're too old for such measures. It's a pity Jack didn't take the time to break you to bridle, my girl."

Before Nell could counter, Dev crushed her against him. The muscles of his arms and thighs were like steel, and his watch chain pressed painfully against her breast. The glitter in his eyes was more pronounced; his voice grated in her ears.

"There are other measures, however," he said, "no less pleasurable to me but, perhaps, more devastating to you. I warn you, Nell. Do not try my patience too far."

"Oh, stuff!" Valiantly, she hid her growing uneasiness behind a challenging look. "What could you possibly do?"

A smile transformed his face, softening its harsh planes. Nell's breath caught in her throat. Just such a smile had, years ago, made her tumble head over heels in love with her father's young lieutenant. Only then he hadn't been angry, else she would have remembered that disquieting gleam in his eyes.

He pushed her away a little. With one hand he cupped her chin, the other slid around her back. His head came down, and his mouth brushed across her lips just as they formed a surprised "oh."

It was over in an instant. Dev walked away, whistling. At the door he turned around. "There are many things I could do," he said, still with that smile tugging at the corners of his mouth. "So don't tempt me, brat."

She stood in the middle of the room and watched him saunter off.

He knew. Perhaps he'd always known that she nursed a hopeless passion for him on the Peninsula.

The insufferable, odious man.

Chapter Seven

Nell was given no time for further reflection, for Wicken appeared, informing her that a Miss Marjorie Simms was below. "The young lady be askin' about yer academy," he explained, his gaze riveted on the battered remains of pink-glazed *petits fours* and the shards of a once beautiful plate of Royal Worcester china—the only one in the dining-room credenza that had not shown a chip or a crack.

"A prospective student? Of course I'll see her," said Nell, who found it cost considerable effort to take her mind off that brief instant when Dev's lips had brushed against hers. "Show Miss Simms into my study. No, better not. I did not finish dusting the books, and they are all over the floor. Show her into the large classroom, please."

"Could have told ye the lieutenant wouldn't like them petty furs. Give an English officer plain old English cucumber sandwiches an' a slice of plumcake, I always say." Wicken turned away. "But would ye listen? Stubborn as a Spanish mule, that's what ye are, Miss Nell."

"I didn't make the cakes for him."

Nell followed Wicken out but stopped in the corridor before ascending to the second floor where the classroom—bare of furnishings save for two frail, worm-eaten chairs retrieved from the attic and a great number of silk-covered cushions strewn about the parquet floor—still resembled nothing more than one-half of a former ballroom.

"And he isn't an officer any longer. In fact, Wicken, he is nothing but an idle fribble, a Bond Street beau, puffed up in his own conceit."

Since Wicken had continued down the stairs to fetch Miss Simms from the small parlor, Nell received no reply. By the time he ushered Miss Simms into the classroom, she had admitted to herself that it was pique at not being able to best the Marquis of Ellsworth during any of their encounters that had driven her to utter such an unfair accusation. Devil Mackenzie might be a Corinthian, a go amongst goers, a man about town, but never a fribble—but he was too bumptious by far.

Thus reassured that she had been correct in at least one of her pronouncements, Nell was able to greet Miss Simms with a welcoming smile and the composure befitting an instructress.

Miss Marjorie Simms was a tall young lady, built on Junoesque lines and with a no-nonsense air about her. She approached Nell with a quick, firm tread.

"You're just as Miss Mofty described you to me," she said decisively. "If you're half as good a teacher as she says, we shall deal famously together."

Nell's eyes danced. "And if you're only half as purposeful as you appear to me, you will undoubtedly be my star pupil. Have you come from Bath, then, Miss Simms?"

"From Tunbridge Wells. Oh, I see! No, I have not spoken with Miss Mofty personally, but I've been in correspondence with her off and on since I left the academy five years ago. Can you teach me about India in two weeks, Miss Hetherington?"

Nell blinked. "Is that all the time you can spare?"

"Yes," Miss Simms said baldly. She eyed the dozen or so silk-covered cushions Nell had spread out in the far corner of the room. A frown wrinkled her wide forehead. "I take it I was not misinformed that in India—if English ladies are invited to a maharajah's palace at all—we are expected to sit on the floor?"

"And expected to remain in the women's quarters," Nell confirmed.

"We shall see about that." Miss Simms walked briskly

across the parquet floor, picked up one of the cushions, placed it atop another, and seated herself rather awkwardly.

"Bend your knees and keep your legs and feet to one side," advised Nell, lowering herself onto a cushion.

It appeared to Miss Simms that her young instructress sank to her knees and sat down in just the prescribed manner, all in one fluid, graceful movement. "By Jupiter!" she said with admiration. "Looks easy enough when you do it, but I fear I can never be as nimble as you."

"It merely requires some practice. I shall teach you the various uses of the cushions by-and-by." Nell pulled another one closer and, with her elbow pillowed on its softness, reclined like a true Eastern lady. "Tell me, Miss Simms, are you headed out for Fort William?"

"Markham—Stephen Markham, my fiancé, you know, is taking up a post in Calcutta, so I daresay I'll see the fort. But we'll not be living there. I may as well tell you straight off that Markham is *not* an army officer."

Nell, encountering a rather belligerent look from Miss Simms, suppressed a smile. As though she'd take offense if one of her pupils did not move in army circles. "Oh? Mr. Markham is with the East India Company, I suppose."

"No. He's taking up a post with Lord Minto at Government House. The position came open rather unexpectedly, and that's why we're in such a scramble to get married. You see, we had planned the nuptials for October, but with Markham scheduled to sail on the second of June—Well, you see how it is."

"It doesn't give you much time, but I don't have very many pupils as yet. In fact," Nell admitted, "you're my first. If that doesn't make you wish you hadn't come at all, I'll be happy to instruct you for as many hours as you can spare."

"Capital. I'm in town for two weeks. Outfitting myself, you know. My aunt and I are staying at Grillon's. I'll come every morning. Shall we say nine of the clock?"

"Bring a list of the items you plan to purchase. I may be able to be of assistance with your wardrobe as well."

Miss Simms nodded and rose with only slight difficulty from her low seat. Nell got up smoothly. She extended her hand, saying, "I'm looking forward to telling you all about Calcutta and a little about India in general. It'll be like going on a flying visit, and I shall enjoy that. Will you be living at Government House?''

''No. Markham is determined to set up his own establishment.''

A little wistfully, Nell remembered the spacious home her parents had rented near the Maidan, Calcutta's beautiful park. Mama had been strong then, glowing with vitality and happiness. It had been the long sea voyage to Lisbon that had sapped her strength, and less than five weeks after their arrival in Portugal, she had died of a virulent fever.

But repining on the past paid no toll. Nell sent Miss Simms a quick, reassuring smile. ''You'll like having your own house,'' she assured her. ''I did. Very much.''

They descended to the vestibule and Miss Simms said, ''I am not generally considered chickenhearted, and I *am* looking forward to the adventure of the long sea voyage. Nothing could be more perfect for a wedding trip.''

''No fear of seasickness?''

''None. But I admit to some trepidation when I think about the native servants I must employ once we arrive in India. I shall take my own maid, of course, but how on earth am I supposed to convey my orders to an Indian cook or to the houseboy, who, I collect, is *de rigueur* and performs much the same services as our footman?''

Nell chuckled. ''There's no need to fret, Miss Simms. Most of the house servants know a smattering of English, and I shall teach you a few words of Urdu. Enough to get by.''

At the door Nell raised her hands, palms together, and bowed from the waist. ''*Namaste*,'' she said.

No slow-top, Miss Simms repeated the ritual before hurrying to the hackney carriage waiting for her in the street.

Nell permitted herself one quick, triumphant glance at Number Two before shutting her own front door. It would have been more gratifying, of course, if the Marquis of Ellsworth had at that moment stepped outside to be withered by her look, but, Nell consoled herself, he would soon enough learn of her great success. Her first pupil. And not a mere officer's bride, but the wife-to-be of an aide to Governor-General Lord Minto.

While Nell was struggling once again with the treacherous kitchen stove in the preparation of dinner, her mind dwelled fondly on the unexpected possibilities opening before her. A recommendation from Miss Simms's fiancé would no doubt bring more business from government circles for Miss Nell's Select Academy, and the East India Company was another client she had not heretofore considered.

The future looked bright, but not so the present, Nell thought morosely as she chewed on a particularly unpalatable bite of the dinner she had carried up to her room. Dev had been odiously right to scoff at her. Cooking in an outdated kitchen was a far cry from sitting around a camp fire to give a spitted chicken a turn while watching her father and his friends at a game of whist. The young officers had never stinted in praise of her efforts when the food was ready to be served and Major Hetherington invited them to take their potluck with him and Nell. She had actually believed herself to be an expert.

Conceding that she had much to learn as yet, Nell returned her almost full plate to the tray. She could only hope that Wicken would not leave in disgust. Without him she'd find herself at a complete stand.

Such a dark mood could not last. The following morning brought not only Miss Marjorie Simms with a very generous fee for the three hours she planned to spend at the academy each day, but also two carters with the chairs and tables Nell had selected at the furniture warehouses for her classrooms. She felt once again on top of the world.

Captain Westcott, arriving in the midst of the bustle to apologize for not having responded to Nell's invitation on the previous day and to invite her for a drive in Hyde Park, received only a distracted look from Nell and a warning from one of the carters to "stand out o' the way, guv'nor!"

"Nell!" Cyprian caught hold of her hand and pulled her to a halt when she would have disappeared up the stairs in the wake of some cane-seated stools. "Surely you're not in a miff that I didn't come to tea? I went to White's for a game of whist, and—well, you understand, don't you?"

"Of course, Cyprian. You decided to make a night of it and probably didn't get back until the wee hours of the morning. Are your pockets quite to-let?" She looked up at him, laughing. "I'm surprised to see you out and about so early."

"'Twas the thought of you, darlin', languishing for my company, that tore me from my cot. Come for a drive?" he said coaxingly. "Fresh air will blow the cobwebs from my head, and we can catch up on our news. How long has it been? Two years?"

"A little longer than that. But I can't, Cyprian. I'm engaged to teach this morning."

"What! Don't tell me that stiff-rumped old harpy carried her little lamb back to this house of iniquity."

"I have a new pupil, and no thanks to you," Nell said with dignity. "Pray excuse me now."

She removed her hand from his clasp, and Captain Westcott had to content himself with a vague promise that she would be happy to drive with him as soon as she had a moment to spare. Piqued, he returned next door, while Nell, not a little pleased and fairly certain that the Marquis of Ellsworth would posthaste be informed of the latest developments at the academy, hurried to rejoin Marjorie Simms.

"How I wish ladies were permitted to gamble at the gentlemen's clubs," she said, entering the now furnished classroom.

"Yes, indeed." Miss Simms closed the book she had been studying on snakes and other poisonous animal life in India. "Ladies tend to play for chicken stakes, whereas the gentlemen do not bat an eye at ten-pound points."

Nell had never played for real money. The fortunes she had won and—very rarely—lost when playing with her father's fellow officers had been purely imaginary ones. She had been excluded when the gentlemen sat down to serious gambling, but her papa had more than once staked his last few pounds on the turn of a card and won.

"I've heard that London ladies send out invitations for select gaming parties," said Miss Simms. "Play at those gatherings is *very* deep."

"Ten shillings a point, perhaps as much as a pound," murmured Nell. Since Cyprian was willing to gamble and lose at White's Club, why should he cavil at losing to her? "Splendid notion. Thank you, Miss Simms."

And Dev. She'd enjoy winning Dev's money.

Nell was burning to put her card skills to the test. She knew she was as good as, if not better than, her papa, who in the heat of winning often had forgotten his own advice to keep a cool head. Nell never lost her head.

Alas, Wicken, whom she sent next door with an invitation, returned with the news that the two gentlemen had left for Newmarket where Dev had a young horse in training for the upcoming races.

Feeling thwarted, Nell spent her afternoons and evenings playing cards with Wicken. No money changed hands, but if it had, Nell would have been "the rich Miss Hetherington" in a very short while.

Her mornings were devoted to Miss Simms. The young lady was an exemplary student, bright, quick, and, most of all, undaunted by the wealth of information Nell threw at her. She arrived punctually, brimful of intelligent questions. Neither was she closed to some of Nell's less orthodox suggestions.

One day she tried on one of Nell's saris. "By Jupiter! This is a capital garment," Miss Simms exclaimed as she turned slowly in front of Nell's dressing mirror. "I shall don a sari as soon as I arrive in Calcutta."

Nell chuckled. "The best part about a sari is that one can shed those awful stays."

"Indeed," Miss Simms said with feeling. "And that rule you advised me of—removing your shoes before entering the living quarters of an Indian home—I think I'll introduce it in my house as well. Always annoys me when my father and brothers, even Markham, stump across our Axminster rugs with stable dirt clinging to their boots."

"I quite see your point, but for some reason or other the rule does not apply to someone wearing boots," Nell said hastily.

Perhaps she had been carried away a little by her eagerness to explain various Indian customs to Miss Simms and had not made it perfectly clear that English gentlemen need not bow to native habits. It was an omission she must speedily rectify if she did not wish to set up Mr. Markham's back. After all, she wanted him to recommend her to other officials setting out for Calcutta with their brides and families.

"In fact, it does not apply to Indian gentlemen either if they have adopted English footgear," Nell said firmly.

"Makes not the least bit of sense to me." Miss Simms, obviously reluctant to give up her notion, unwrapped the sari from her stately figure and allowed Nell to assist her into her walking dress of striped percale. "Well, I must be off to the apothecary's. Markham wishes to take an ample supply of quinine."

Nell accompanied Miss Simms into the street. As on previous mornings, a hackney coach stood waiting, and Miss Simms's aunt was peering anxiously through the dusty glass-pane in the carriage door.

Marjorie Simms extended her hand to Nell. "I shall be sorry when our lessons come to an end," she said. "Never thought I'd enjoy myself so much. You've made me look forward to my stay in India and allayed my fears. Markham says he's proud of me, but it's you he should be proud of."

Nell watched the coach disappear around the corner of Chandos Street into Cavendish Square. She, too, was enjoying herself. She had never had a female friend—except for her mother, who had always treated her more as an equal than a daughter. Marjorie Simms, with her frank and open manner, might have been just such a friend. But in little more than a week Marjorie would return to Tunbridge Wells, and then—

Resolutely, Nell dismissed such morbid reflections. New pupils would flock to the academy. Wicken had collected two letters at the post office earlier in the morning. One from Miss Mofty, alerting Nell to a visit from Lady Olivia, the Earl of Clapford's daughter. Lady Olivia planned to be married in September to Lieutenant Viscount Wolverton and was toying with the notion of accompanying him to Spain. She was very interested in Miss Nell's Select Academy. The second letter had come from Kent, announcing the imminent arrival of Bess Wainwright, who was pleased to come to chaperon Nell.

Nell turned back to the house. She had just mounted to the top of her front steps when the door of Number Two opened. Dressed for riding in buckskin breeches, a coat that looked as though it had been molded to his muscular frame, a black hat, and shiny black boots, the Marquis of Ellsworth stepped outside.

So, he had returned from Newmarket, had he? Nell gave him a covert look. She had not seen him since he threatened to spank her but instead had embraced and kissed her. And she had not missed his company. Not one bit. Except that he'd been unavailable to play cards.

"Miss Hetherington." He doffed his hat with flattering promptness. She could not fault his bow, yet there was something about his greeting, perhaps the habit he had of laughing at her with his eyes, that caused her to regard him with wariness and to bid him a very curt good morning.

He shook his head at her. "Not a good morning at all," he said dolefully. "And it's you who cut up my peace."

Not deceived by his mournful tone, Nell raised a brow. "What have I done now? I caused no ruckus this morning. I did not fire a pistol. No carter bumped furniture against the wall."

"Worse, Nell. What am I to do about you?"

Instantly, she bristled with indignation. "You can do nothing at all about me. I own this house, and you may as well stop trying to oust me."

"But will my conscience permit me to stand by while you instruct an innocent young lady in a most improper manner?" The disconcerting gleam in his eyes deepened. "Advising her to *discard her stays*. Nell! I was never more shocked in my life."

For a moment Nell was speechless. Her face flamed with embarrassment. He had eavesdropped on what had been meant for Miss Simms's ears alone! Anger welled up in her. She took an impetuous step toward the separating rail.

"You are without shame, Devil Mackenzie! A gentleman would have removed himself from the vicinity instead of listening in."

One dark brow rose in astonishment. "What! Leave my own chambers half-dressed because two giddy girls are indulging in a most improper conversation? What rubbish you talk, Nell."

Her hands gripped the iron rail between them. "So," she said, fighting for control over her temper. "Your bedchamber is right next to mine. I shall have to take care what

I say in my room so as not to put you to the blush again, my lord.''

The corners of his mouth twitched upward. "Actually, there's a dressing room between our chambers. My window was open, however, and knowing you, I assume yours was open as well.''

She nodded. Unthinkable to sleep behind closed windows. She could move into the middle bedroom, but then Bess would have to sleep right next to the dividing wall. There were also the two tiny maids' rooms next to the stairs. . . .

His deep voice, brimming with amusement, broke into her thoughts. "You still rise to whatever bait is cast your way, don't you? But if I promise not to tease you anymore this morning, will you come riding with me?''

Her eyes flew to his face. To be riding again for the first time in over two years—it was too good an opportunity to miss, especially if the offer included the use of one of Dev's mounts. Even in Portugal and Spain he had owned the most magnificent horses.

"Will you mount me on one of *your* horses?''

"I saw you race against Cyprian, remember? Would I dare offer you a livery hack?''

Her last doubts dissipated. "Done," she said, turning to go inside. "Sixpence to a groat that I'll be changed in less than five minutes.''

"I never bet on certainties." Dev vaulted over the low railing. He followed her into the house, saying, "Take all the time you need. I'll just have a word with Wicken. Is he belowstairs?''

Already halfway up to the next floor, Nell called over her shoulder, "In my study.''

True to her word, she was changed in a very few minutes. If Dev recognized her riding habit as the one she had worn in Portugal and Spain, he made no comment, only offered her his arm as they stepped out of the house and walked to the stables in the mews.

Dev's stallion, a powerful roan with a vicious look in his eyes, was already saddled and held by two grooms hanging on to the reins. Nell cast a longing glance at him, but a quick peep into Dev's face persuaded her not to ask if she might ride him. She chose instead a spirited chestnut mare called Pepper.

As they traversed the long stretch of Oxford Street leading to Hyde Park, Nell had ample opportunity to congratulate herself on her choice. Pepper, although chomping at the bit and dancing with impatience to run, was a very well behaved lady and responded perfectly to Nell's slightest command. The stallion, on the other hand, was not above rearing or kicking his hind legs at some hapless vendor's cart, and if Dev had not reined him in with an iron hand, he would undoubtedly have raced on at a full gallop. He made it perfectly clear that he was king of the road, and no beast or vehicle had the right to go before him.

"I knew you could handle a horse, but I never realized what a nonpareil you were until I saw you on this brute," Nell said as they entered the park by way of Cumberland Gate.

Dev grinned, tipping his crop to the brim of his hat. "May I return the compliment? You still have the best seat of any woman it's been my privilege to see on a horse."

"Thank you." Feeling quite in charity with him, Nell turned her mount toward the west, where the park lay deserted and it was unlikely that they would encounter barouches and landaulets filled with starchy matrons out for an airing. "Let's reward our patient mounts."

So saying, Nell dug her heel into Pepper's flank and raced across a grassy stretch toward a stand of trees about a half-mile distant. The air was still and, away from streets and traffic, filled with the perfume of flowering shrubs and trees. As Pepper picked up her pace, the pungent scent of pines mingled deliciously with the sweeter smell of plane trees and fanned her cheeks.

Hoofbeats drummed behind her. Laughing, Nell urged her mare to greater speed. She'd had no doubt that Dev would follow. He was like her in that he could not resist a challenge. She'd had no doubt either about the outcome of the short race. But it mattered not one whit. It was the exhilaration, the tiny spark of hope that perhaps she might win after all, which made racing so exciting.

As Dev's stallion thundered past, Nell made one last effort to reclaim some of the lost ground, but the mare was no match for the powerful roan. Nell reined her in a little and watched critically, as Dev brought his horse around the first trees, then pulled him to a halt.

"Well done," she said, riding up to Dev. "You have him beautifully schooled. Oh, if only I had a mount to match him, I'd give you a race you wouldn't forget. What do you call him, Dev?"

"Master."

She broke into a peal of laughter. "Buttering him up sweet? But I doubt not he knows who is the master."

"He knows, when *I* am on his back," said Dev with a note of warning in his voice. "If I ever catch *you* trying to ride him, I will wring your neck—if he hasn't broken it by the time I find you."

"Unfair, Dev. Will you forever throw it in my face that I once made off with your horse? And how could I help it when Cyprian said I could not win against him? You yourself assured me that only one of *your* horses could beat his Sheik."

"Did I indeed?" Dev set the stallion in motion. "How careless of me. I should, of course, have added 'with me in the saddle.' "

Nell compressed her lips. She *would* have won had the stupid horse not stepped into a rabbit hole and stumbled. She had held him up beautifully, too, and had not been more than a nose length behind Cyprian. But she should have known that the mood of easy camaraderie between her and Dev could not last. He must always say something to put her down.

An expression of sardonic amusement flitted across Dev's harsh features when he encountered Nell's smoldering look. "Come now," he said. "Is that the thanks I get for giving my grooms the order to saddle up the mare whenever you wish to ride? How do you like her?"

Nell's eyes widened in astonishment. "Do you mean it, Dev? If you knew how much I miss riding! You can have no notion—" She broke off in confusion under his look. It was warm and full of understanding.

Her face burned. "Thank you, Dev," she said quietly.

"Don't mention it. I never ride her, and she's been eating her head off, getting fat and lazy in the process. A little exercise will do her good."

"I know I should not accept, but I *cannot* bring myself

to refuse.'' Nell gave him a quick look. She thought she had guessed who had last ridden Pepper, so obviously a lady's mount. But why he did not have the mare taken to Josephine's new establishment, she could not imagine.

"Pepper is beautiful. Although, for my taste,'' she said, a twinkle of mischief dancing in her eyes, "she could be a mite stronger.''

"Minx!'' It crossed his mind—and by no means for the first time—that Jack Hetherington's little girl had grown into a most charming young lady. With those wide gray eyes laughing up at one, a man had to be mighty careful not to lose his head. And her soft mouth with its tantalizingly short upper lip—*dash it! Kissable, that's what it was*.

Under his scrutiny, the kissable mouth grew prim and the clear eyes kindled with a light he had no difficulty recognizing as suspicion.

"Why are you doing this?'' she asked. "Why are you being kind to me when you want to drive me out of London?''

"Not out of London. Only out of my house.''

"It is *my* house.''

"Fane House,'' he said, compromising.

"Why are you letting me ride your horse?'' Nell drew Pepper to a halt.

Good manners dictated that he stop as well. Having no clear-cut answer to that perfectly logical question, he knitted his brows in the most repressive frown he could muster. It was intolerable that she should question his motives. He had made the impulsive offer, and she must take it or leave it.

"Nell,'' he said severely. "You are the most exasperating—''

"Oh, look!'' Her face brightened, and she waved her riding crop excitedly at three horsemen who were cantering up. "There's Anthony Marple with Giles Fairfield. They taught me to shoot rabbits. Do you remember, Dev, in Portugal—''

"I remember,'' Dev said dryly, torn between gratitude that he need not continue his bluster in lieu of a rational explanation, and exasperation that the officers would undoubtedly tell her how wonderful they thought her crazy scheme of opening an academy for officer's brides. "Who's the third?''

"Brigade-Major Hugh Chadwick," she said softly.

Dev did not miss the warmth in her voice and eyes and gave the third officer a sharp look. He had no trouble recognizing the sunburnt major who had suggested at White's that Nell should be invited to sup at the Piazza after a visit to the theatre.

"For heaven's sake, brat," he said harshly. "Remember your position. Don't fall around their necks, and, above all, don't invite them to the house until you have a chaperon."

Chapter Eight

Nell had time only for an exasperated look at Dev before the riders drew to a halt beside them.

"Nell! By all that's wonderful!" Lieutenant Anthony Marple, freckle-faced and ruddy under a thatch of red hair peeping from beneath his shako, pressed his mount close to Nell's mare. "We heard of your school. Will you permit us to call on you?"

"Will you ask us to a game of whist?" Giles Fairfield, the youngest of the three, broke in impetuously. "Remember, Nell? Soult interrupted us in the middle of the rubber. And we were winning, too!"

Laughing, she agreed to receive them and to play whist. Then, while Anthony and Giles greeted Dev, she turned to Major Chadwick, a tall, lanky man of about forty, who had served in India with her father.

"Hugh, I did not realize you were acquainted with Giles and Anthony. Have you been transferred?"

"Aye. Soon's my furlough is up—which will be in ten days, thank God—I'll be on my way to join old Hooknose on the Peninsula. But tell me about yourself, Kitten."

His use of her mother's pet name for her and the familiar sight of the lazy, indulgent smile creasing his swarthy countenance brought a lump to her throat. Hugh Chadwick was a link to the past, to the happy times before she and her parents had sailed for Portugal.

While she struggled for composure, Hugh said in his teasing way, "Still a hoyden, I see. Has no one told you a lady don't gallop in Hyde Park?"

"For shame, Hugh." Nell opened her eyes wide at him. "Don't tell me you've turned Methodist. Besides, there was no one around to observe me."

"We saw you, didn't we? That's what brought us over here. Only female I know to ride neck or nothing is Nell Hetherington." Then, looking at her rather intently, he said, "Nice little mare you're riding there."

Nell patted Pepper's sleek neck. "The Marquis of Ellsworth was kind enough to lend her to me."

"Ellsworth?" Major Chadwick directed a hard stare at Dev, who kept himself in the background and appeared to be absorbed in the management of his nervous stallion. He favored Dev with a curt nod. "Knew I met you before. Week ago at White's, wasn't it? Preached propriety to us when we planned to take Nell to a play. Said she needed a chaperon. Yet you, apparently, may ride with her and no groom in sight."

Nell's eyes flashed. More interference from Dev. How dare he! She tugged on the reins, turning her mare to face him.

"I suppose," Anthony Marple said with an accusing look at Dev, "you planned all along to steal the march on us."

"On the contrary. I tried to prevent your making a byword of her." Dev's cool glance encompassed the three officers. "Somebody has to look after the chit."

"Dev, you had no right," Nell said angrily. "My door is always open to my friends."

Hugh Chadwick removed his penetrating stare from Dev. "Ellsworth a relative of yours, Kitten?"

"Lud, no! He's a neighbor who wants to make my life in London intolerable so that I'll sell him my house. But I will not sell, and if you allow him to dictate what you may or may not do, why, then—"

"Easy now, Kitten," Hugh said soothingly. "What about this chaperon business? I cannot believe you'd flout the conventions and live by yourself."

"You *have* turned Puritan," Nell said in a voice that clearly denoted her disappointment in him. "Set your mind at rest. My chaperon arrives tomorrow."

"In that case, I'll give myself the pleasure of calling on you," Hugh replied, a twinkle in his hazel eyes.

Dev's mouth tightened. He nudged his stallion. "Shall we ride on? Which way are you headed?" he asked Anthony Marple, who brought his mount around to fall in step beside Master.

"Planned to meet Plymm and Stewart at the Life Guards, but I daresay they won't mind if we don't go with them. We'll ride with you and Nell."

"You don't mean it, Tony!" Giles Fairfield's smooth young face registered shock. "Not go! Why, Stewart assured me this promises to be the best turn-up of the century."

Anthony Marple shrugged and laughed. "What a boy you are, Giles. Surely a ride with Nell rates higher than a prizefight?"

Giles blushed and looked at Nell. "You understand, don't you?" he said imploringly. "Gentleman Jackson will referee the match, and Stewart believes that Cribb will come as well."

"Of course you must go. All of you." Nell urged her mare into a trot. "After all, we were just about to turn home, weren't we, Dev?"

"Were we?" His face was inscrutable, but she thought she detected a flicker of surprise in his eyes.

Had he expected that she'd try to talk the boy out of watching a prizefight? As though she were as scheming as he. Telling her friends they mustn't take her to a play, the finagler.

With Giles Fairfield and Hugh Chadwick flanking her,

Nell drew ahead. Summoning a smile, she asked Ensign Fairfield, "When is your furlough up?"

"Tony and I are not on furlough." Giles's chest swelled with pride. "We're under special orders from Lord Wellington."

"Congratulations. That is quite an honor. But, in that case, I don't suppose you'll be in London long."

"We'll probably sail on the thirty-first of May with the same transport as Major Chadwick. That is," the young ensign added morosely, "we will, if those stodgy fellows at the War Office are done in time with whatever it is that they're supposed to be doing for Wellington."

Absently, Nell patted her mare's sleek neck. "There'll be the devil to pay if he doesn't get what he wants. I was only a child when he campaigned against the mahrattas in India, but I remember well how cutting he could be."

Nell and Major Chadwick became absorbed in reminiscences about India, and for a little while she forgot about Dev's high-handed behavior. Giles Fairfield, impatient to be off to the prizefight in a certain field near Hounslow, spurred his mount and pulled ahead of them.

When the Life Guard barracks came into view, Hugh Chadwick broke off his account of a tiger hunt in Bengal. He looked at Nell as though he'd been hit by a flash of inspiration. "I say, Kitten, did you perchance pick up the lingo when you were in the Peninsula?"

"Well, yes. I already knew some Spanish, of course, which made it easy for me to become quite fluent. And Portuguese, after all, is not much different."

He gave a snort. "*You* may think so. I daresay others won't."

"Shall I teach you?" Very much aware of Dev riding with Anthony Marple a short distance behind them, Nell shot a challenging look at Hugh Chadwick. "I'm not very expensive, I promise, and you'd be surprised how much you can pick up in ten days."

White teeth flashed in his dark face. "What would your fair pupils say if I were to attend your Academy for Young Brides?"

"Rest easy. I have only one so far, and she is learning Urdu. I'd take good care not to put the two of you together."

"By Jove! I'll take you up on your offer. When do we start?"

One of the two riders behind them increased his pace. Nell did not look back. "Come tomorrow afternoon."

"Nell!" Dev said harshly. "Are you out of your mind? If setting up your academy isn't bad enough, must you ruin yourself completely?"

Turning in the saddle, she gave him a cold look. "Bess Wainwright will be with me tomorrow."

"What's that to the point?" Dev fell in on her right-hand side. "She'll never want to sit in on your lessons. Bess Wainwright and learning, indeed!"

Major Chadwick leaned forward, directing his lazy smile at Dev. "Come now, Ellsworth," he said across Nell. "Aren't you rather gothic in your notions?"

Dev's hand tightened on the reins.

"If Nell's mother didn't see anything wrong with her daughter teaching me Urdu, why should *you* object to her helping me with a few phrases of Portuguese and Spanish?" asked Hugh.

Nell frowned at her old friend. "Don't bother to justify yourself, Hugh. Neither you nor I require his permission for—"

"This, Chadwick, is London." Dev's voice had a bite to it that wiped the smile from the major's face. "What may be permissible in Calcutta will not be tolerated here."

Nell shot a black look at Dev. "You're an intolerable, pompous—"

"Tell me, Ellsworth," Hugh demanded. "What's your interest in Nell?"

Both men drew their horses to a halt. Nell, after glaring from one to the other, shrugged her shoulders and rode on. It mattered little, one way or the other, *what* Dev's interest might be.

"The interest of a friend of Jack Hetherington's," she heard Dev say with hauteur and, despite her proclaimed in-difference, was assailed by a twinge of pique.

"So was I a friend of her father," Hugh retorted.

Anthony Marple joined Nell. "What did you say to set them against each other?" he asked. "They look like a pair of fighting cocks."

Nell reined Pepper in and glanced over her shoulder. The two men were still staring at each other. Hugh challenging, Dev tight-lipped with anger.

"I'd say they look like a pair of dowagers trying to outstare each other."

"Dowagers?" Anthony said in mock horror. "They're worse than fighting cocks. Permit me to retreat from the battle zone." He raised his shako and rode off, chuckling.

Nell hardly paid attention. Her eyes were on Dev and Hugh. She wasn't at all sure how she felt about their proprietary attitude. And, dash it, if they hadn't learned yet that she would do as she saw fit no matter what they said, then she'd be well rid of both.

Dev's stallion broke the tension between the two men when he pawed restlessly and strained against the bit, frustrated because he could not bear to see Pepper ahead of him. Reluctantly, Dev set his mount in motion. Hugh followed suit.

"About time, gentlemen," Nell said sharply. She pointed her crop toward the Life Guard barracks. "Are those your friends, Hugh, meeting up with Giles and Anthony? I'll bid you good day, then."

Hugh gave her a two-finger salute. "When shall I see you tomorrow?"

"Two o'clock?" She watched Dev's face. He looked as though he wanted to protest, then changed his mind. Unaccountably, she was disappointed.

"Two o'clock, Kitten." Hugh started toward his friends. "If that knight of yours doesn't run me through before then."

Nell scowled, but Dev made a sound that was suspiciously like a snort.

"Kitten, indeed!" he said. A reluctant grin lifted a corner of his mouth. "Anyone less like a kitten I have yet to meet."

Her eyes on the officers riding off in a cloud of dust, Nell said, "If you mean that I'm not helpless and soft, you're undoubtedly right."

"Surely Chadwick is aware of that as well. So why does he call you Kitten?"

"If you must know," she said, less than gracious, "my

second name is Christina, and since Papa had wished for a boy, he used to call me Kit when I was a youngster. Mama changed it to Kitten, and after Hugh twice rescued me from a tree, he took to calling me Kitten as well.''

''And you're still going out on a limb. Nell, Nell! Will you never learn?''

He looked unbearably smug. His words and voice mocked her, but worse, she could not think of a crushing reply. Nell pressed her heel into Pepper's flank, urging her into a canter. She'd had enough of riding, at least in Dev's company.

How he got under her skin with his moralizing, his barbed remarks about the impropriety of her behavior! Devil Mackenzie, who had completely disregarded proprieties by installing his mistress in his great-aunt's house.

Not a word did she exchange with Dev on the ride back to Chandos Street. Instead, she occupied herself enumerating the many instances when he had, with sublime disregard of her wishes or her feelings, interfered in her life.

But, unless she moved out of her house—perish the thought—she was saddled with him for a neighbor.

In front of Number Two-A, Nell slipped off the mare's back before Dev could guess her intention. She handed him the bridle. ''It's late. I fear I do not have the time to return Pepper to the stables. If you would be so kind?''

''Will you be riding tomorrow?''

''I don't know yet.''

Dev's mouth tightened. ''Send me word. Since you don't have a groom, I'll ride with you.''

Nell glared at him. ''How kind.''

She picked up the wide skirt of her riding habit and marched up to her door. It closed after her with a quiet deliberation that seemed ominous to Dev. A slam to shake up elegant Chandos Street would have been more reassuring. It would have given vent to her spleen.

For a moment he sat lost in thought, frowning at the door as though it could reveal to him the mischief Nell must be brewing. She had fairly bristled when she learned that the warning he'd uttered at White's had kept her friends from paying a visit. And when he tried to thwart her dumbfool notion of teaching Hugh Chadwick, his efforts had merely stiffened her resolve. As if she did not realize how quickly a young lady could lose her reputation.

He nudged his stallion toward the mews. What a stubborn, contrary girl she was. Dashed if he knew why he bothered to prevent her more foolish starts. If she disgraced herself, she would have to leave London for sure and he could buy her house.

Mayhap, if he hadn't known her as a skinny little kid, hadn't witnessed her valiant struggle to overcome her grief at her mother's death, instead giving Jack Hetherington the comfort and support he needed. Mayhap, if she weren't so different from young ladies of the *ton*. Starting her own school, by George!

Clearly, since Nell had become his neighbor, the stifling boredom he had suffered after selling out had completely left him. He hadn't been tempted to seek Josephine's new love-nest, nor had he made an effort to secure the cooperation of one of the birds of paradise who made up the chorus lines at the Opera House.

In fact, he had no time for his former amusements. When he wasn't rushing off to Newmarket to check on his horse, he was kept busy checking on Nell.

Concealed behind the drapes in the small downstairs parlor, Nell watched as Dev, with Pepper in tow, clattered along Chandos Street, then disappeared in the narrow alley-way that led into the mews.

She sank down on the cushioned bench in the bowfronted window embrasure. Dev was an insufferable meddler, taking advantage of his friendship with her father. His purpose was clear. He wanted to drive her out of Number Two-A. Perhaps, as he said, to restore Fane House to its original greatness and splendor. Perhaps to reinstall Josephine. It was a lowering thought.

Nell tossed her head. She could not care less what was his final goal. She was determined to thwart him, and she'd wager a pony that she would succeed. This house—half of a house—was the foundation of her independence. No one must take it from her.

And yet, if routing her was Dev's purpose, why was he placing Pepper at her disposal? Knowing that she wouldn't be able to afford the hire of a horse for Wicken, he had even offered to accompany her on her rides.

Why, if he wanted her out of the house, had he sent his footmen to remove her trunks from the landing and store them in the attics?

But at the same time, Dev also pointed out that her lack of servants precluded her establishment in London. She couldn't possibly live without a cook, he said, or without an abigail.

Her chin tilted at a decidedly obstinate angle. She would show him how very wrong he was. She *would* have her school. She *would* teach Hugh Chadwick. Perhaps, she'd even make her curtsy in society with Lady Lansdowne's help.

On those uplifting thoughts, Nell took herself off to the kitchen to struggle once again with the preparation of dinner. Wicken, coming from the cellars with a basketful of wood for the stove, watched her efforts to dress the half-dozen crabs he had bought at the Billingsgate market.

"Miss Nell," he said after a moment. "It's not four o'clock yet. When are ye planning' to eat?"

"I had no luncheon, Wicken. Do you expect me to last until six?"

"In town, dinner is served no sooner than eight o'clock," Wicken replied severely. "And if ye think that Mrs. Wainwright will be happy with yer scramblin' way of livin', ye had best think again or look for another companion. I r'member the lady well. A bit giddy perhaps, but a stickler nevertheless."

Nell snipped sprigs of parsley and some chervil. "I promise we'll dine at eight tomorrow night."

"And forget about the stove," advised Wicken. "Use the old furnace if ye plan to have roasted ducklings tomorrow."

Nell wiped her hands on the voluminous sacking-apron she had tied over her gown and went to peek into the large whitewashed chamber next to the kitchen. She was full of misgiving as she eyed the brick furnace with its antiquated ovens and huge spit.

"Do you think you'll be able to light a fire under the spit?"

"And why wouldn't I, Miss Nell? Haven't I lit yer camp fires come rain or hail or thunderstorm?"

"Yes, but—"

Looking once more at the cavernous opening that contained the spit, Nell banished her doubts. She knew she could roast ducklings over an open fire. Had done so more than a dozen times. With a delicious chestnut stuffing, too.

"Very well, Wicken. The spit it is. And when Mrs. Wainwright has settled in, I'll invite the marquis and Captain Westcott to dinner. A dinner that *I* shall cook. I'll show him that I am capable of fending for myself."

Wicken shook his head. He had no need to ask whether it was the marquis or the captain she wanted to impress.

The following morning, Nell awoke to overcast skies and the threat of rain in the air, but nothing could dampen her spirits. She had found a second goal—one that might even rate above her school. She would prove to the Marquis of Ellsworth once and for all that she was her own mistress, and woe to him who dared interfere.

Engaged in daydreams, which always ended with Dev begging her pardon and assuring her that he had never known a more resourceful lady than Nell Hetherington, she settled in the breakfast parlor with coffee and toast. Dev would admit that she was no longer the scrawny girl of the Peninsula. He would look at her with warmth and approval and tell her that she was beautiful. More beautiful than Josephine.

Her cheeks stung with shame and a quick burst of anger—anger directed at herself. She did not care whether Dev thought her beautiful. She did not care if he ever kissed her again. No longer was she the silly, besotted little fool who would have given her eyeteeth for one of his dazzling smiles, for a look of admiration from his deep blue eyes.

Now, she told herself firmly, she wanted only his respect and his admission that she was capable of making her own decisions.

Wicken came into the room and handed her the mail he had collected at the receiving office. She broke the seals and scanned the contents of the three missives, two of them bills.

Nell stifled a groan. How little it took to shatter her dream of gaining Dev's praise. She let the two bills drop onto the not-yet-paid-for tablecloth. "What dratted nuisance!"

Without ceremony, Wicken picked up one of the sheets of vellum. "From Manton's." He squinted a little to make out the figures set down by the gun-maker's clerk. "Fifty-five guineas for a brace of pistols bought on the fourth of May. Aye, that's correct, Miss Nell. I picked 'em up just afore I came here."

"I know. But, Wicken—" She looked at him, consternation reflecting in her wide gray eyes. "Fifty-five guineas?"

Wicken pulled out a chair and sat down. His gaze fixed unwaveringly to her face, he spoke slowly, as though addressing the child Nell, whom he had cosseted and protected for so many years. "Now, Miss Nell, what's this all about? Didn't ye know how much a pistol would cost ye?"

"No."

"Then why not make do with yer own little pistol? Why did ye order two more?"

Confronted by his sternness, Nell grew uncomfortably warm. "I was so sure I'd have at least a half-dozen pupils, all of them paying me an attractive fee."

"Ye were so sure! Miss Nell, how often have I heard those words from ye? An' how often were ye wrong?"

As though Wicken had not spoken, she said, "And all of them would have to be taught to handle firearms. Why, even Miss Simms, who has frequently hunted with her brothers, admits that she doesn't know one end of a pistol from the other."

"But ye don't have any pupils *but* Miss Simms."

"Yes, I do. Captain Chadwick has asked me to teach him Spanish and Portuguese."

Chapter Nine

For a moment Wicken was speechless. His weathered face turned a shade darker. "Miss Nell," he spluttered. "Surely ye're not thinkin' of teachin' a *male* at yer academy for ladies!"

Nell countered his look of outrage with one of defiance.

Shaking his head, Wicken grumbled, "And I thought ye had it all planned nice an' proper when ye wrote about the house an' asked me to buy the pistols an' to come work for ye. I should've known better."

"Well, mayhap you should have," retorted Nell. "But that is no reason to sound so odiously like Dev—like the Marquis of Ellsworth. Let me remind you, Wicken, that I am a grown woman. I know what I am doing. And if I make a mistake, I'll know how to set it to rights."

Wicken stared at her from beneath bristling brows. "And ye sound just like Major Jack. I'd like to know what ye want them new pistols for? Teach a crack shot like Major Chadwick?"

The question hung between them, unanswered. Wicken nodded with gloomy satisfaction. "There now," he said. "Let's see what else ye got in the post."

"Wicken, you're incorrigible." Nell couldn't help but smile at him. "It's only a bill from one of the furniture warehouses for the cane-seated stools, and the other is a note from Mr. Forsythe."

"Does he say anything about money?"

"No. And I didn't expect him to. He says he'll be attending Lady Lansdowne tomorrow morning and will call on me afterward."

"Miss Nell?" Absently Wicken scratched the stump of his arm. "Mayhap ye should consider the lieutenant's offer?"

"He's not a lieutenant any longer," Nell said sharply. "And I would not consider his offer, even if I had to choose between it and debtor's prison. So don't speak of it again."

She pushed back her chair preparatory to rising. "One more thing, Wicken. Don't bother fetching the mail. I can wait for the postman to deliver my bills in the afternoon. And now let's think no more about this. If I must, I'll return the pistols."

Despite her brave words to Wicken, the bills preyed on Nell's mind. Soon, more would come: bills for tables and two couches, for sheets, towels, and table linen, not to mention the outstanding accounts with the butcher, the greengrocer, and various other shopkeepers. But she hadn't run aground yet. As long as she paid a little something on account, the merchants would be satisfied. That was what Papa had always done, and it had worked splendidly for him.

She must, however, have more pupils. Soon. Else she'd find herself at very low tide indeed. If Dev hadn't behaved in such an odious manner while Mrs. Margood and her daughter were present, she'd already have *two* pupils. Three, counting Hugh Chadwick.

Nell's hands were busily preparing the second bedroom for Bess Wainwright, but she hardly spared a thought for her friend traveling up from Kent this very day. Her mind was preoccupied with such weighty matters as a lack of funds, a lack of pupils, and a surfeit of the Marquis of Ellsworth.

She felt she'd be able to deal with him much better if only he wouldn't, just when she least expected it, do something kind or smile in such a way that reminded her of the brash young officer to whom she had lost her youthful heart. Not that they were much older now. She had yet to turn twenty, and Dev was her senior by only seven years. The problem was that in Devil Mackenzie's eyes she had been a pesky little girl in Spain when, in fact, she had been a young lady of seventeen summers.

He still did not acknowledge that she had grown up. And he wanted her house.

Nell was not unhappy when, at this point in her ruminations, she heard Miss Simms talking to Wicken on the floor below. Her lessons with Marjorie would effectively put Devil Mackenzie out of her mind. Too often lately, she had spent more thought on how to prove to Dev that she was a young lady than on a feasible scheme that would keep the house permanently in her possession. This must stop.

While Nell and Marjorie Simms immersed themselves in the mysteries of nasal vowels, semi-vowels, and unaspirated consonants of the Urdu language, Dev came whistling down the stairs on the other side of the dividing wall. Still whistling, he entered his breakfast parlor, a snug little room overlooking the gardens.

Unlike Nell, Dev could afford payment for early delivery of his papers and mail, and, as usual, Salcombe had placed a stack of gilt-edged invitations, letters, and copies of *The Times* and the *Morning Post* beside his coffee cup.

"A letter from His Grace," the butler pointed out as though Dev wouldn't recognize his grandfather's ducal seal.

"Thank you, Salcombe. Please send word to the stables that I shall require the curricle at ten o'clock."

Dev broke the wafer and scanned the terse message penned in bold black strokes. His Grace, the Duke of Stanford, respectfully requested—*respectfully, by Jove!*—the presence of his grandson at Stanford Hall in Hertfordshire to discuss the matter of Augusta's bothersome heir. At Dev's earliest convenience. "Earliest" was twice underlined.

A bark of laughter escaped Dev. His Grace would have to be content with a letter from his dutiful grandson. At present, he had no intention of leaving Nell to her own devices.

Still chuckling, he opened one of the pieces of mail that had the distinct look of a bill. As he perused the linendraper's precise accounting and polite request for payment, Dev's good humor vanished.

Mr. Soames, linendraper, had sold a dozen sheets and pillowcases, two dozen towels, and one Irish linen cloth with napkins to Miss Nell Hetherington and bold as brass charged the items to the Marquis of Ellsworth. Likewise, a second bill informed Dev, Miss Hetherington had purchased two upholstered couches and four tables with marquetry work from Sadler's furniture warehouse at the corner of Longacre and St. Martin's Lane.

"The deuce!" Dev muttered. "The girl has gone stark raving mad."

Did she suppose he'd fork out several hundred pounds to furnish her house? *His* house before long. And then it'd be furniture from Stanford Hall that would grace the restored Fane House, not some frippery modern couches.

Ignoring the handsome stack of invitations, Dev thrust back his chair. With the bills clutched in his fist, he stalked off to confront Nell with her debts and his opinion of her backhanded dealings.

He tore open his front door, then stopped in his tracks. Never had he known Nell to work in a backhanded manner. She had always been honest and forthright. Although more than two years had passed since he last knew her in the Peninsula, he did not believe she had changed all that much.

Absently, he closed the door, retraced his steps to the breakfast parlor, and stood for a long time at the window overlooking the small patch of garden behind his house. Beyond the low brick wall that divided his half of the garden from Nell's, he saw Wicken pinching dead blooms off a peony bush. The empty sleeve of his left arm had come untucked from his coat pocket and dangled uselessly at his side.

Deep furrows creased Dev's brow. When Jack Hetherington's batman had opened the door of Number Two-A that first morning after his invasion of Nell's bedchamber, he hadn't given a second thought to the strangeness of finding the old soldier acting as butler. Wicken had always looked after Nell in the Peninsula. But, surely, he could not have been with Nell in Bath. She must have approached Wicken after she arrived in London.

Dev's frown deepened as he realized that Wicken was probably one of the many crippled wretches who, no longer of use to His Majesty's armies, had been discharged and thrown upon the mercy of their families. Or, if they had no family, condemned to beg in the streets.

And when Nell would finally give up her crazy scheme of starting a school, Wicken might be back on the streets.

"Hell, no." Dev pushed away from the window. She had only to accept his offer. She'd be able to pay proper wages to Wicken *and* to a maid.

He looked at the sheaves of paper in his hand. It took him a moment to channel his thoughts back to the question why he found himself saddled with Nell's bills. Soames and Sadler. The more he thought about it, the more familiar the names seemed.

On impulse, Dev went into his study across the hall. He pulled open the drawer of his oversized mahogany desk that contained his ledgers. Selecting a volume from the previous year, he started flipping through the pages. It didn't take him long to find the entries he was looking for. They were marked in green to show that the expenses had been incurred on Josephine's behalf.

Furniture from Sadler's and linens from Soames's. Obviously, the two merchants had somehow or other come to the conclusion that Nell was Josephine's successor.

A slow grin lit Dev's face. How furious Nell would be when she found out about the mix-up. He could see her, sparks shooting from her gray eyes, and condemnation of his character—she would not hesitate to blame *him*—pouring forth from her mouth. A most inviting mouth. Since that brief moment when he had captured her lips for a punishing kiss, he wanted nothing more than to repeat the experience. But not as punishment.

Drumming his fingers on the polished surface of the desk, Dev considered what he should do. She was a proud little thing. Perhaps she'd be more embarrassed than furious. It was a thought that took the pleasure out of showing her the bills.

He was considering his options—return the bills to the merchants or pay them—when Cyprian stuck his head in the door. "Aren't you ready yet, Dev? Tattersall's, remember? Forsythe is auctioning off his grays."

A gleam leaped into Dev's eyes. It was not caused by anticipation of the blood-horses he'd inspect at Tattersall's but by the recollection of another Forsythe. His late great-aunt's solicitor. Now Nell's.

He'd hand the bills and money to Mr. Forsythe and let him settle the matter discreetly.

"Let's be off. The curricle should be at the door." Dev rose. "But don't make any engagements for the afternoon," he warned. "You must take my place chaperoning Nell at two o'clock. I find I have an errand in the city at that time."

As they left the house he omitted any mention of the particulars of his errand, explaining only that Nell had foolishly offered to teach Brigade-Major Hugh Chadwick at her academy.

"And she doesn't seem to understand that she'll ruin herself," he added in a fresh burst of irritation. "If it became known that she spends the better part of an afternoon in his company—begad! It doesn't bear thinking of."

"I take it, he's a ramshackle fellow, this Chadwick?" asked Cyprian. "I say!" He stopped on the flag-way and looked from the curricle to the threatening sky. "Might be better to take the closed carriage."

Dev paid no attention to the fine drizzle or to Cyprian's suggestion. Cudgeling his brains for a means to impress upon his friend that Hugh Chadwick was more than a mere ramshackle fellow, he climbed onto the seat and took the reins from his groom.

"I don't trust Chadwick," he said, keeping to himself that his mistrust arose mainly from his knowledge of the captain's long friendship with Nell—he called her Kitten, the bounder. Worse than that, Nell's eyes and voice betrayed that she was not indifferent to the major, who was old enough—well, almost old enough—to be her father.

With a flick of the reins, Dev set his pair of bays in motion. "The major," he said grimly, "must on no account be left alone with Nell. Do you remember Lisbon? The two beauties who escaped their duennas and offered to show us the sights?"

A grin stretched Cyprian's face as he remembered the amorous adventures enjoyed with the two enterprising young damsels, but the grin was speedily replaced by a scowl. "Yes, indeed!"

"Nell is expecting her chaperon today," said Dev. "But knowing Bess Wainwright, I shouldn't be surprised if she forgot that she's supposed to come to London."

"Trust me. I'll make damn sure Chadwick won't be alone with Nell."

Dev was not totally reassured, but he said no more. Having served with Cyprian Westcott in the Peninsula under Lieutenant General Sir John Moore, he was well aware of his friend's sterling qualities. Whether Cyprian would be able to stay Nell in one of her more headstrong starts was another question altogether, but at least his presence would make it impossible for Chadwick to take advantage of Nell's naivete.

That Nell was naive and inexperienced, Dev did not doubt for a moment. Her total lack of suspicion when he had put his arms around her, and her look of surprise when he brushed his lips against hers, had given her away. She was an innocent, a babe among wolves, and she must be protected.

But it would not be Major Chadwick who'd be Nell's protector.

At Tattersall's, Dev paid so little heed to the horses put up for auction that Cyprian raised a brow. "If you ask me," he said with a broad grin, "you may as well admit that Nell has caught your fancy. I've never seen you fret over a female as you do over her."

"Don't be daft." Dev shot him a scornful look. "She's a dashed nuisance. That's why she's preying on my mind."

Cyprian's comment, however, had the salutary effect of turning Dev's attention to the business at hand: the buying and selling of horseflesh. For an hour he discussed and argued the finer points of thoroughbreds, none of which caught his fancy sufficiently to make a bid.

They returned to Chandos Street and sat down to luncheon just as the occasional morning showers changed to a veritable deluge. Dev knew a moment's temptation to put off his visit to the solicitor. However, he ordered his carriage out for half past one—the closed carriage, despite the fact that his coachman would take twice as long for the journey to Lincolns Inn Fields as Dev would have taken in the curricle. Nell's solicitor must on no account see him as Devil Mackenzie, a young blood careless of dignity and appearance. Mr. Forsythe must be confronted by the Marquis of Ellsworth, a proud, haughty peer, whose only purpose was to rid himself of a couple of bills without embarrassment to himself or to the young lady who had incurred the expenses.

In his pearl gray greatcoat and curly brimmed beaver hat atop his chestnut locks, a gold-tipped walking stick in one hand and a pair of finest leather gloves in the other, Dev looked indeed every inch the elegant man-of-the-town as he set out.

He turned to Cyprian, who accompanied him to the front door. "Mind you don't make a mull of it. We don't want Chadwick to know that we suspect him of wanting to seduce the child. Only want him to understand that we're concerned about her reputation."

"If you don't think I'm able to handle it, chaperon her yourself," said Cyprian, wondering how two or even three officers in Nell's drawing room could be better for her reputation than one. "Surely you can postpone your business in the city."

"No."

Cyprian shrugged and opened the front door. "Hope you won't regret it," he said darkly. "If Nell starts teaching officers as well as officers' brides, you'll lose your wager for certain."

Dev had, in fact, forgotten about his wager with Cyprian, but that was not an admission he'd make voluntarily. He whisked outside into the streaming rain and made a sprint for the protection of his carriage.

He should never have made that bet with Cyprian. What with one thing or another, he had been far too busy protecting Nell from her own foolishness to work on a scheme that would oust her from Number Two-A before the month was out.

Dev had never lost a wager. But now, with the month of May more than half over, it looked as though he might lose this bet. Because of Nell. And she wasn't even grateful for his efforts to save her reputation.

Resentment kindled in his breast as his carriage rattled through the cobbled streets. Absently, he fingered Nell's bills. If two merchants made the mistake of sending their accounts to him, more, perhaps, would follow suit. To spare Nell's blushes, he would again and again visit Mr. Forsythe, fork over his blunt with instructions to pay on Nell's behalf and, in general, make a bloody fool of himself while the headstrong young miss established her blasted school.

The deuce, he would! He'd fork over his blunt all right, but he'd make damn sure the bills remained in his possession.

Dev's mouth curled in a devilish grin. He had hit upon a means to put the bills to good purpose. A purpose that would help him win his wager after all.

With his glove, he cleared a patch in the fogged coach-window and searched through sheets of rain for familiar landmarks. The coachman was taking an unconscionably long time getting to Lincolns Inn Fields. They were only just entering Holborn, but Dev could hardly wait to see the solicitor.

It was raining hard when Marjorie Simms left Number Two-A shortly after noon. Nell thought with compassion of Bess, traveling on what must be the wettest day of the entire spring season, but it was not until Hugh Chadwick burst into her foyer at two o'clock, shaking torrents of water off his military cape, that Nell began to realize just how late Bess was.

"Hope your chaperon has arrived," Hugh said in greeting. "I'd hate to think I got soaked for nothing."

"Oh," said Nell, feeling as though she should have arranged for sunshine on this momentous day to celebrate that she had garnered a second pupil and a companion. "I suppose the rains delayed her. Bess is driving up from Kent, somewhere near Chatham."

"Nell, you wretch!" Hugh tossed his cape over the banister and set his dripping shako on the tiled floor. "Under good conditions that's a five-hour drive, six if the lady don't care for speed. And no lady is ever ready to start a journey before noon."

"*I* would not wait until noon," Nell said indignantly. "I'd start out at seven or eight."

"You're no lady. You're a hoyden." Hugh looked at her dispassionately. "But you've grown dashed pretty. Ellsworth is right. You shouldn't receive gentlemen unchaperoned. Particularly not a reprehensible officer of His Majesty's army."

"And you accused Dev of being gothic. Devil a bit, Hugh! You're absolutely medieval."

He grinned. "Mind your language, Kitten. One would think you'd grown up in a camp. But I really mustn't stay. Be a good girl and fetch me a drop to warm my innards and to fire my waning courage for the next charge into the elements."

"You may have a glass of Madeira. But I'll not serve it to you on the doorstep."

"Where is Wicken? I understand he's nursemaiding you again."

Nell started up the stairs. "His niece brought us a bite of luncheon from her mother's chophouse. He's taking Peggy back to Orchard Street. Come along now. The wine's in my study."

Hugh Chadwick had no chance to follow Nell. The knocker rang against the brass plate. Nell cried, "Bess!" and went flying down the stairs again, pushing past Hugh and throwing open the door with a flourish.

Her face fell when she saw Captain Westcott standing on the stoop. "Cyprian, I'm afraid this is not a good time for a visit."

"I say! You might ask a fellow in." Cyprian Westcott stepped inside and shut the door. "The portico is not watertight, you know."

"You don't look wet."

"Nell, my darlin', I hope you don't take me for a slowtop. I don't relish a soaking any more than the next, so I jumped over the rail."

"I wish you'd jump right back. I am busy." Looking as though she would have liked to put him out with her own two hands, she remained stubbornly by the door. "If you like, you may come back later and drink a cup of tea with Major Chadwick and me."

With an elaboration that could not fail to catch attention, Cyprian raised a quizzing glass to his eye and surveyed Hugh. "Cyprian Westcott, at your service. Are you the officer Dev sent me to watch?"

"Sir!" Hugh Chadwick pushed away from the stairs, but Nell motioned him back.

She directed her most ferocious scowl at Cyprian. More meddling from Dev. It was not to be borne. "If Dev sent you to play propriety," she said coldly, "you may tell him to go to the devil. I shall brook no interference from him."

"Tell the devil to go to the devil?" Cyprian grinned, then leveled the quizzing glass at Nell. "It appears, though, that he was right. I seem to have arrived in the nick of time."

"In time for what?" Nell's indignation wavered at the sight of Cyprian's enlarged eye. Her mouth quivered. "Put that glass away. Where on earth did you get that monstrosity?"

"Borrowed it from Dev. To quell the major's pretensions."

"Now, see here," said Hugh, the tone of his voice icy, the set of his jaw and his clenched fists leaving no one in doubt as to his feelings. The narrow entryway seemed suddenly too small to contain the two men. "I can take your insults, Westcott. But what you're saying also casts aspersions on Nell's character. An arm in a sling won't protect you if you persist in this slander."

Nell stepped between the men. She was quite in sympathy with Hugh, but a mill on her premises she did *not* need. "Cyprian, if you don't behave, I shall quell *your* pretensions in a way you won't appreciate at all."

Cyprian laughed and allowed the glass to drop. It dangled from its black satin ribbon to lie, incongruously, against the pale blue and gold of his hussar uniform. He bowed to Hugh Chadwick. "Ellsworth sends his regrets," he said smoothly. "He'd have come himself, but some unexpected business took him into the city."

"Why would Ellsworth have come?" asked Hugh, his swarthy countenance turning darker still. "I didn't expect him, and neither, I take it, did Nell. So, why does he trouble himself sending his totally unnecessary regrets?"

"He feared you might be uncomfortable, Chadwick. That you'd miss your lesson rather than compromise Nell if the rain delays Mrs. Wainwright's arrival."

Again, Nell's temper flared. If Dev were present, she'd favor him with her opinion of his character, but wretch that he was, he had stayed away.

She did not hear Hugh's reply to Cyprian. She only knew

that she wanted to punish Dev. He was determined to disrupt her school. And when he could not do so himself, he didn't hesitate to use Cyprian against her. That was something she would not forgive.

Neither would she forget that Cyprian allowed himself to be used. He, too, deserved punishment. She was familiar with his weakness for young ladies of the muslin company and knew just how to make him regret his ill-advised meddling.

"Dev had business in the city?" she said mockingly. "Poor Cyprian. Dev certainly pulled the wool over *your* eyes."

Cyprian frowned.

"Carlton House to a Charley's shelter," Nell said with a smugness purloined from Dev's repertoire of annoying expressions. "Dev has a tryst at the Covent Garden Theatre or some such house of diversion. He's no doubt seeing a ladybird he doesn't want you to meet. So he sent you on a fool's errand."

"Oh, no. You wrong him," Cyprian protested, but he looked less than certain, a fact that did not escape Nell.

Perhaps Dev had, indeed, gone to seek the diversions of one of the high-flyers of the muslin company. If so, she could not care less. And that hollow feeling in her chest was due to relief. Having Dev ensnared by an opera dancer was better than having him underfoot. Indeed.

"Since you're here, Cyprian," she said, whirling to go upstairs, "I suppose you may as well serve your purpose. You can brush up your Spanish and teach Hugh some of the phrases only a man would know."

She led the way to the second floor, but her mind was not on Spanish lessons. She was rehearsing a few choice English phrases she'd hurl at Dev when next he showed his face at Number Two-A.

Chapter Ten

It was not to be supposed that Nell's first lesson with Hugh turned into a success. In a belated attempt to minimize the presence of a male at her ladies' academy, she had chosen her study as the place of instruction. The cozy if timeworn chamber was furnished with a battered desk pushed beneath the only window, four easy-chairs, a fireplace surmounted by a carved oak mantel, and bookshelves covering one wall and the narrow spaces on either side of the door. Surely it was a place to make any gentleman feel at home.

Hugh, seated at the desk with Nell, remained oblivious to the study's charming qualities. He showed himself irritable and impatient when Nell explained some of the vagaries of the Spanish language. And Nell, who had successfully dealt with a gaggle of disinterested girls in Bath and could claim unqualified success for her lessons with Miss Simms, felt unaccountably ill at ease.

Only Cyprian Westcott, lounging in a deep leather chair in front of the narrow fireplace, seemed happy with his lot. But then, he did no more than flip through the pages of a book of engravings while Hugh struggled with verbs and nouns of a foreign tongue.

Every so often Cyprian would thrust the poker into the grate, where several logs burnt in a desultory fashion, or bestow a careless glance upon pupil and teacher. It was, no doubt, that occasional look, so carefully schooled into blandness, which contributed to the air of restraint hanging over Hugh and Nell. She, at least, was convinced of it and without hesitation apportioned the blame to Devil Mackenzie, who had sent Cyprian to play chaperon.

Barely half an hour had passed when she pushed aside her Spanish notes. "I have a mind to play cards. Let's continue our lesson tomorrow."

Hugh was not unwilling. "But mind you have a proper chaperon. Ellsworth must be queer in the attic if he believes Westcott can fulfill that role. In fact, you shouldn't let any man set foot inside the house until Mrs. Wainwright arrives."

"I'll have Wicken guard the door." Nell shot him a dark look. How priggish he had become. In fact, both Dev and Hugh were dead bores with their constant preaching of propriety.

From a desk drawer she took a pack of cards, rather the worse for wear from her practice sessions with Wicken, and started to shuffle. "What's your pleasure, Hugh? Piquet?"

"I say!" Cyprian closed his book. "Aren't you going to include me in the game?"

"You don't deserve it, Cyprian, but I suppose we could play three-handed whist. I warn you, though. Hugh never plays for fun. A shilling a point is his minimum."

"Not when I play with you," protested Hugh. "If you must lose your money to me, let's make it penny points."

"A shilling," Nell said firmly, her mind on the sums of money she planned to win from Cyprian and Dev.

Cyprian pulled his chair against the narrow side of the desk opposite Hugh and, withdrawing his arm from the sling, declared himself ready for action. They settled down to some serious playing, interrupted only when Hugh got up to light the lamps, or Cyprian, complaining about the smoking fireplace, stirred the embers and added another log.

"You should have the chimneys swept," he said, picking up his hand. "I doubt not you have a starling's nest or two up there."

"I'm sure you're right. All the fireplaces smoke. Even the kitchen stove." Nell played the ace of spades, took the trick, and led with her queen of hearts.

The game was going well. She might be able to afford a sweep. But, dash it! In all likelihood the ill-drawing chimneys were Dev and Josephine's fault. No doubt they had carelessly neglected the house's maintenance.

Resolutely, she put smoking stoves and fireplaces from her mind. "When you're gaming," her papa used to say, "don't waste a thought on anything but the cards in your hand and those already played. Especially when you want to win."

Nell wanted to win.

Shortly after four o'clock Wicken entered and reminded her that she ought to prepare the syllabub and dress the ducks for the dinner she had planned for Bess Wainwright.

"Oh, all right," said Nell, taking the last trick of the game. "But I'm beginning to wonder if Bess decided to stay home until the weather changes."

Cyprian gave her a sidelong look. "Dev believes she forgot she was to come up today."

"Fustian." With admirable restraint, Nell forbore to vent the more forceful terms that sprang to mind, describing her view of Dev's beliefs. She turned to Hugh, who was busy totting up the score. "What do you make it, Hugh? Did I win?"

"You won all right." Tossing down his pencil, Hugh looked at her with awe. "Confound it, Kitten. You even beat me. When did you learn to play? In Calcutta, you didn't know a spade from a club."

"Didn't do nothin' *but* play cards in the Peninsula," muttered Wicken, who still hovered in the doorway. He saluted Hugh Chadwick. "Good to see ye, Major. Daresay ye hardly reckernized our Miss Nell."

"Matter of fact, I had no trouble at all. She's still a hoyden. Only change I could detect is that she's no longer scrawny."

"How much did I win?" Nell interjected impatiently.

Hugh looked at his tally. "Eight pounds and two shillings. What about that wine you promised earlier? I'm sure Captain Westcott could use a drop. He went down heavier than I did."

"If ye don't mind comin' into the kitchen?" Wicken held the door invitingly. "I might be able to find a glass of brandy for the both of ye."

Nell whisked out the door. "Wicken," she said with a

severity belied by the twinkle in her eyes. "You make very free with my brandy. First you serve it to Dev, and now you offer it again without so much as a by-your-leave. I think I had better take charge of it myself."

In the kitchen, Nell invited Hugh and Cyprian to sit at the scrubbed table. She made herself a cup of tea, then, while the two officers sipped their brandy, blended thick cream, lemon, sugar, Madeira, and frothed the mixture in a chocolate mill.

"What are you making?" asked Hugh, watching with fascination as she ladled off the rising froth and placed it in a hair sieve to drain.

"A whipped syllabub," Nell replied absently. "Wicken, did you light the fire under the spit?"

"Nay, but I'll have a good blaze going afore ye can say tinderbox." Wicken marched off into the furnace room next to the kitchen.

Frowning with concentration, Nell spooned the drained froth into glasses that had already been half-filled with red wine. She stood back to admire her efforts. "Looks pretty, doesn't it?"

Cyprian chuckled. "Never did understand why the ladies absolutely devour their syllabub after a good dinner. Until now."

"Awful, sweet stuff," said Hugh. "Still don't see why they like it."

"It's how they get their wine, old man. Without seeming to drink a lot."

Wicken came stamping back into the kitchen. "Miss Nell," he said, rubbing his forearm across his soot-smeared face. "Something's wrong with that there danged furnace. Can't get anything out of it but a belch of smoke."

"I knew this place was going to rack and ruin. Now what am I to do?" Arms akimbo and a belligerent look on her face, Nell advanced on the brick furnace.

Hugh followed. "Let me have a look. Perhaps the damper is closed." Warily he eyed the monstrous furnace whose outdated brick ovens loomed above an open spit large enough to roast a calf or a fair-sized pig. He stuck his head into the cavernous opening where Nell planned to roast two small ducks for dinner.

"Seems all right," he said, emerging with a soot mark on the tip of his nose. "Perhaps the logs are wet."

Cyprian, not to be left out, shouldered Hugh aside. "Let's have an expert take a look."

"Oh, leave it be," Nell said crossly. "I wouldn't be surprised if Dev had the chimney bricked up and didn't tell anyone about it."

"Why would he do that?" Cyprian removed several logs and piled more kindling into the grate. "He doesn't own the place—yet."

"And he never will!" Nell countered fiercely. "But he used to rent this house for his mistress, and I wager he was too much of a nip-cheese to pay the sweep."

"There! What did I say? It's burning." Cyprian reached for a log but was forestalled by Hugh.

"Allow me. It's all right to play cards with an injured arm, but lugging wood is overdoing it."

Nell coughed. "Leave it be. Don't you see you're getting more smoke than fire?"

"I'll take care of that." Cyprian pushed open the small casement windows set into the thick walls on either side of the huge furnace.

A gust of wind and a spray of raindrops swept into the chamber. Flames shot up around the piled logs, then died down.

Hugh shook his head. "It's no use. Best give it up."

"Nonsense. What we need is more draft. Wicken!" Cyprian shouted. "Open the kitchen windows and the back door."

"In India the natives light fires with cow dung and grease," offered Hugh.

Exasperated, Nell said. "Unfortunately, we have no cow dung in Chandos Street."

"Surely you have some grease?" Cyprian took up the poker, thrusting it into the smoldering kindling. "Wicken!" he shouted again. "Bring newspapers and grease."

"Oh, for heaven's sakc!" Nell clamped her mouth shut as Wicken, with deplorable promptness, responded to Cyprian's command. It was no use saying anything. Building a fire beneath the spit had become a matter of honor to the three men.

They worked hand in hand, Wicken forming loose wads of paper, Hugh dunking them in a pot of grease, and Cyprian stuffing the obnoxious mess among the kindling. Soon Nell was not the only one afflicted with a cough. At times she could barely see the men through the fog of smoke wafting through the room and burning her eyes. Still, they heaped more paper and kindling onto the pile.

Seized by a fit of irrepressible coughing, she was about to retreat from this chamber of torture when she heard Cyprian say, "We've almost got it, men. Hand me the grease. I'll pour it over the logs."

"No!" cried Nell. She rushed toward Cyprian, but through the open windows tore a blast of wind and a great quantity of rain, slicking the tiled floor. She slipped and would have fallen had Hugh not clasped her around the waist and steadied her.

"Easy now," he said just as Cyprian scraped the last of the grease into the tiny darting tongues of flame. "I think that's done the trick."

And, indeed, two or three flames shot high, taking hold of kindling and logs. Another gust of wind fanned the flames, dispersing them until all of the wood was alight. The smoke grew thicker. It still did not go up the chimney but drifted toward the windows, which were, unfortunately, too small to accommodate the heavy clouds. The fire also tried to follow the path to air and started licking the brick mantel.

With dawning horror, Nell saw a huge flame leap at the wooden shelf affixed to the brick where, no doubt, cooks of the previous century had kept pots, pans, and ladles.

"Put it out!" she screamed. "My house! You're burning down my house!"

She had not seen Wicken leave the furnace room, but he appeared at her side with a bucket of water from the kitchen. Hugh grabbed it and tossed the water into the grate.

Hissing and spitting, the fire dimmed—only to revive with greater force and belching clouds of black smoke.

"Get outside." Again Hugh's arm clamped around Nell's waist.

"No!" She struggled to free herself. "We must put out the fire!"

"The house won't do you any good if you're dead of suffocation," said Cyprian, grabbing her hand.

Followed by Wicken and pursued by black, stifling smoke, Cyprian and Hugh half pushed, half dragged Nell from the basement kitchen. But even on the ground floor the smoke was thick, forcing them outside. Coughing, their eyes streaming, the trio emerged into the street.

"I fear you were right, Nell," said Cyprian. "The chimney is bricked up."

"But nothing much will happen to your house," Hugh assured her. "The fire will burn itself out without our help."

She did not reply—could not for fear of bursting into tears or a torrent of abuse. If her house were to burn down, she'd *never* forgive any of them.

Shaking off their restraining hands and arms, she turned to face her home. She felt neither rain nor wind as she watched smoke drifting out the open front door and smoke rising from the kitchen windows in the rear.

She did not see the crowds gathering behind and beside her, nor did she hear Cyprian's mumbled offer to fetch her cloak. She only knew that she might lose her house. Her independence.

Damn you, Dev! If you bricked up the chimney . . . !

The visit at Mr. Forsythe's office on the first floor of Number Five, Arab Row in Lincolns Inn Fields, took longer than Dev had anticipated. For one thing, the heavyset man in the old-fashioned frock coat, who should have been cool and businesslike, came near to having an apoplexy when he learned the reason for Dev's visit. Neither did he instantly grasp the roll of banknotes Dev held out to him with instructions to call on the two merchants and pay the bills in Nell's name.

Mr. Forsythe had a great many impertinent questions to ask the Marquis of Ellsworth, and Dev was hard-pressed to come up with satisfactory explanations. He not only must explain his involvement with and his interest in Miss Nell Hetherington, but must do so in a manner that did not give away his somewhat nebulous schemes of revenge upon Nell.

It was no easy feat, and a less determined man might have given up. Not Dev.

Finally, after wrangling with his stubborn conscience for close to an hour, the solicitor agreed to accept Dev's money for the merchants and promised to keep the transaction from Nell.

"You won't regret it, I promise you," said Dev, suppressing his elation beneath a winning smile and a hearty handshake.

Mr. Forsythe accompanied Dev to the door of his private office. "Maybe I won't and maybe I will," he said cautiously. "But I say this to you, my lord! If I learn that something havey-cavey is going on, my word to you is null and void. I'll pay the bills myself before lending my services to any underhanded scheme of yours."

"Believe me, Mr. Forsythe, I have no underhanded scheme in mind," Dev said. And if he spoke more calmly and more soothingly than might be expected from a man accused of harboring dark and sinister designs on an innocent young lady, Mr. Forsythe gave no sign of suspicion.

"Besides," Dev added for good measure. "Miss Hetherington would thank you even less than she would me for laying out the money on her behalf."

The solicitor nodded. After all, he'd had a glimpse of Nell's determination and drive for independence when he saw her in Bath. With more cordiality than he had shown before, he bid his visitor good-bye, adding, "You'll have to tell her eventually, you know. She's bound to wonder why the two merchants never sent her an accounting."

Chuckling, Dev stepped into the outer office. "I take leave to doubt that, Mr. Forsythe. Nell is too much her father's daughter to fret about a bill she never received."

He donned his cloak held out to him by one of Mr. Forsythe's clerks. Whistling under his breath and twirling his walking stick, he descended to the ground floor. The bills rustled in his pocket. Two pieces of crisp paper that would place Nell in his power if he so chose.

His coach was nowhere in sight; only Chester, his groom, lounged in the shelter of the doorway. The wiry, middle-aged man snapped to attention. "I took the liberty, my lord, ter send old Jeff to the Swan Inn ter shelter the horses. I'll fetch 'em now."

Dev glanced at the rain, which was pouring as if from gigantic buckets. He pulled up the collar of his cloak and pressed his curly brimmed beaver down firmly. "Nonsense. Do you think I'll stay here kicking my heels in this damned doorway when I could be enjoying a drink while the horses are harnessed?"

Without the benefit of the oilskin slickers worn by his groom and coachman, Dev was drenched to the skin by the time they reached the Swan Inn. He ordered ale for his groom, then toasted the success at the solicitor's office with two glasses of cognac, and five minutes later was on his way home.

Dev's carriage was solidly built and virtually draft free due to the lavish use of interior paneling and thick velvet hangings. Even so, he was soon chilled through in his sodden garments that clung to him like obstreperous seaweed, and with every turn of the wheels he grew colder and more disgruntled. The burst of elation he had experienced in the solicitor's office became but a faint memory.

If he did not wish to present himself with chattering teeth at Number Two-A, he'd have to change before checking up on Nell. The devil fly away with her. No doubt she was cozily installed before a fire and playing three-handed whist with Cyprian and Major Chadwick. Nell would be fleecing the men. She was a devilish-sharp player.

Or, perhaps, Bess Wainwright had arrived and made a fourth. Bess, the scatterbrain. Pity her partner. A corner of his mouth lifted in wry amusement but dropped again as a fresh wave of chills swept his body.

The moment his coach entered Cavendish Square, Dev caught an aura of excitement. For a miserable day such as this, far too many servants were rushing around in the square. They shouted and gesticulated. Uneasily he noted that they all ran north, his direction, toward Chandos Street.

He heard the ominous clanging of a fire engine. His coach slowed, then stopped altogether. Chills and clammy garments forgotten, Dev tore open the door and jumped down. The cobbled street was slick and treacherous with puddles that hid rutted and worn stretches, but heedless of danger

Dev rushed ahead, past his carriage and the crowd of surging footmen and hall porters.

Through the gathering dusk and gusting rain he could see the fire engine ahead, a huge monster with three pumps, pulled by six plodding horses. A dozen or more men wearing the yellow hats and badges of the Sun Fire Company ran alongside and another dozen had found footholds on the engine and clung to pumps and hoses as the contraption rumbled and rattled toward its destination.

Dev ran faster. Passing the fire engine, he sprinted into Chandos Street. Smoke drifted out the open front door of Number Two-A, and more big black clouds billowed from the garden side of the house.

Nell again.

She stood surrounded by Wicken, Cyprian, Hugh Chadwick, and a knot of curious bystanders in the street in front of her house. Her muslin gown was plastered to her body, her hair hung in long wet strands down her back, and she was arguing fiercely with Cyprian, who held out a cloak in his uninjured arm and tried in vain to place the protective cover around her shoulders.

Grim-faced, Dev watched her slap away the cloak. Really! Cyprian should know better than act the chivalrous knight with that willful female.

"Will you leave me alone!" she shouted as Dev came within earshot. "Dash it, Cyprian! Haven't you been helpful enough when you built the fire under that infernal spit? And who the devil called the fire engine?"

She whirled away from Cyprian Westcott and came face-to-face with Dev. "You!" she said with loathing. "I've been waiting for you."

Chapter Eleven

Nell's attack came so unexpectedly that Dev was bereft of words. Perhaps he had misheard. It wouldn't be surprising with the rain drumming on the cobbles and the flag-walk, with men shouting, a female or two screeching, and the fire engine coming to a noisy halt in front of the house.

But there was no misunderstanding the fury blazing from Nell's eyes and the angry tilt of her chin. He could think of only one reason for her outburst. She must have learned of the bills.

Impossible. She could not know.

"And I cannot wait," he said, including Wicken, Hugh Chadwick, and Cyprian in a grim look, "to get you away from your friends. So that I may wring your neck! What are you trying to do, Nell? Burn down my house?"

"It is *my* house. And besides," Nell added with as much belligerence as indignation, "if it burns down you have none to blame but your own cheese-paring self."

"You're daft. What did you do? Try to light a camp fire in your sitting room?"

The barb fell on deaf ears. Nell was already too angry and upset to take offense at a mere wisecrack. Raising herself on tiptoe, she glared at him. "Did you or did you not have the chimney in the furnace room bricked up?"

"You lit the old furnace?" His brows snapped together.

"Why, you little fool! Those ovens haven't been in use since my grandfather and Augusta were infants."

A small army of firemen brushed past them, some going around to the back of the building, others disappearing into the smoke-filled house, while the rest of the crew hauled ladders and lengths of leather pipe off the engine. Nell did not notice. No longer did she stand on tiptoe. No longer did she glare. Her eyes, wide with dismay, were raised to Dev's face.

"They haven't been used?" she asked in a hollow voice. "Not even the spit?"

"No."

Wicken cleared his throat and muttered something about wanting to see what the firemen in the house were up to. He melted away, followed by Hugh Chadwick. Cyprian, after a moment's hesitation, thrust Nell's cloak at Dev and rushed into the house as well.

"I suppose I should have realized that," Nell said wearily. "What cook would use such antiquated equipment?"

She raised a hand and brushed a strand of wet hair off her forehead. Raindrops beat against her upturned face and streaked down her cheeks. Like tears.

Something stirred in Dev. A tenderness he had never experienced before. A warmth that started in the region of his heart and spread until his whole body was affected. Anger and resentment fled before the wish to comfort, to assure her that everything would be all right.

He laid his hands against her cheeks and with his thumbs wiped away the moisture. Lud! He wanted to kiss her.

Her eyes widened, and instantly Dev let his hands drop.

Just maudlin, he told himself. Because he couldn't bear the thought of Nell crying. He had seen her break down only once. At Coruña, when the commanding officer had ordered her to join the wounded aboard the transports before her father and the many other dead had received a burial.

In any case, she wasn't really crying. It was the rain that made her look vulnerable.

"Come now," he said gruffly. "Nell Hetherington admitting she's made a mistake, that's something I never expected."

She did not reply, just looked at him as though she had received a shock far deeper than the fire or his small gesture could have caused.

Or, possibly, she had anticipated a thundering scold and did not know what to make of his forbearance. Well, he could deal with that. He flung the cloak around her shoulders and marched her onto the flag-walk. "We're in the way. The firemen must pull the pipe into the house, you know."

Nell gave a start. "What!" she squealed. "Surely they're not going to pump water into my house! Hugh said the fire would burn itself out."

She whirled, raced up the front steps past swearing firemen encumbered with the unwieldy leather pipe that would convey water from a drum carried on the fire engine, and disappeared in the entryway.

Dev stared after her. The tender feeling that had engulfed him less than half a minute ago wavered but did not quite dissipate. Interfering little ninnyhammer. He had better go and keep an eye on her. If she wasn't careful, she'd upset the firemen. There was no telling what they'd do when their dander was up.

In a few long strides he was inside the foyer. The smoke was not half as thick as it had been when he arrived in Chandos Street, and he had no difficulty seeing Nell huddled in the space beneath the stairway.

"How dare you!" she cried, but Dev knew that for once her ire was not directed at him. She was addressing the back of a fireman, a great hulk with shoulders like a prize-fighter and fists the size of hams. He stood planted between her and his crew as they pushed and dragged the leather pipe toward the back stairs.

"How dare you snatch me up and put me aside as though I were a chair or a vase," she said furiously. "I tell you, there is no fire! It's just a bit of smoke."

Dev grinned. He wished he'd been quicker and seen the giant pluck Nell off her feet and set her out of the way.

Her hands balled into fists. "Let me pass!" she commanded, but that wall-like back was unresponsive.

Dev thought it time to intervene. He did not put it past her to pummel and hit as much of the fireman as she could reach. She'd be in the suds then, especially if there was no blaze to be put out and the men believed themselves cheated out of their reward money.

"Nell, behave yourself." He eased his way through the knot of yellow-hatted men crowding the entrance hall. "Don't you know how lucky you are? The fire brigade arrived as promptly as anyone could wish. And the smoke's gone."

"*I* know that," she said, turning her indignant gaze on him. "But do *they* know the smoke's gone? I don't want them to—"

A shout from the doorway interrupted her. "Ready to use them pumps!" a fireman yelled just as Cyprian ascended from the kitchen and reported that the fire had burned out in the grate.

The hulk in front of Nell finally stirred. "Well, then," he said with a challenging look at Nell. "Well, miss?"

Her color deepened. "*Well*!" she mimicked. "You may leave, sir. And take your water pipe with you!"

The men in the hallway eyed Nell with hostility. An angry mutter arose, filling the narrow space, drawing those firemen who had gone down into the kitchen area.

It dawned on Nell that, perhaps, all was not well with the extinction of fire and smoke. She remembered reading in one of the London papers to which Miss Mofty subscribed that the set-up of fire brigades had turned out a mixed blessing for Londoners. Rival companies had been known to fight for the privilege of dousing a blaze while the building in question burned to the ground.

Most vividly, however, she remembered an incident concerning an inn somewhere in the city. The fire engine had been summoned, but the blaze had been put out by the proprietor and his staff before its arrival. Believing themselves wronged, the firemen had entered the inn. Shouting, "Fire! Fire!" they had tossed every stick of furniture out the windows and started the pumps, dousing the chambers until their water drums ran dry.

If the men of the Sun Fire Company were to indulge their pique and man the pumps, soaking her furniture, her walls and floors, she might as well give up her plans for the school. She simply did not have the funds for refurbishing.

A chill ran over her body. She ascribed it to her dripping wet gown beneath the cloak Dev had draped around her. Nell Hetherington did not shiver with apprehension.

Facing the giant fireman whose yellow badge looked to her like some monstrous eye watching her every move, she realized she couldn't afford *not* to pay the men something, even though they had done no more than clutter up her entrance hall.

"I appreciate your prompt arrival," she said with no outward sign of the fear and indignation churning in her breast. "If you'll excuse me for a moment, I shall fetch a purse."

The angry muttering among the men ceased, but not one of them stirred to remove the threatening leather pipe from her house. More than a dozen pair of eyes watched closely as she started to go upstairs—as though the firemen suspected she might try to abscond.

She met Dev's gaze and hesitated. He nodded encouragingly. For an instant she believed she saw again that glow of tenderness that had taken her breath away earlier and had brought about a shocking revelation of the true nature of her own feelings.

As she stood looking at Dev, his air of encouragement changed to one of impatience. He advised her to shake a leg unless she wished to detain the men of the Sun Fire Company for no good reason at all.

Calling herself sharply to order, Nell hurried on to the third floor. She was not so foolish as to believe that the danger of having her belongings soaked was over so long as the firemen were still in the house, but she did feel safe while Dev was keeping an eye on them. He might want her removal from Number Two-A more than anything in the world, but he would do his utmost to prevent the Sun Fire Company from driving her out.

In her bedroom, Nell opened the strongbox she kept in the deep recesses of her wardrobe. Carefully, as though they were golden guineas instead of crown pieces, she counted out ten coins, letting them drop one by one into a chamois pouch. Taking a deep breath, she counted out ten more, and then another four silver pieces. Twelve pounds; a large chunk of her meager savings. Surely it was enough to pacify the firemen.

As she descended to the second floor, she became aware of the acrid smell in the house. The smoke might be gone, but the odor lingered, growing stronger with each downward step. She grimaced wryly. A perfumed welcome, indeed, for Bess. But, then, Dev might be correct, and Bess had forgotten that she was supposed to be traveling to London.

Realizing that she was sinking into a morbid, self-pitying mood and was, moreover, doing Bess Wainwright a grave injustice, Nell increased her pace. Scatterbrained the young widow might be, but she would *not* forget that her friend needed a chaperon.

Dusk was falling rapidly, steeping the corridors and stairs in gloom. Nell stopped by her study to pick up the lamp Hugh had lit during their card game. Her winnings still lay on the desk. Eight pounds and two shillings.

Her eyes brightened. She wasn't all that much out-of-pocket after all. Less than four pounds. She could easily make it up in another game.

She resumed her descent, and as she approached the ground floor she saw that all but the huge fireman had left. The leather pipe was gone as well. She did not see Wicken or Hugh, but Dev and Cyprian were ushering the large man from the Sun Fire Company to the door.

Jingling a handful of coins in one hand and doffing his hat at Dev with the other, the fireman said, "Thank 'ee, guv'nor. I call this mighty generous. A guinea a head, and two extra yellow Georges for settin' the little lady out o' harm's way."

One foot suspended in midair, Nell came to an abrupt halt on the stairs. So Dev had paid them off. He must think her incapable of settling the matter.

It was worse than that. Dev had his back to the stairs, but when he spoke, she could hear a grin in his voice.

"You misunderstand, my friend. The extra money is not a reward for what you did, but for the enlightenment your action gave me. I finally know what to do with the lady when she proves obstreperous."

The fireman shrugged and walked off, but Cyprian said, startled, "I say, Dev! You're not referring to Nell, I hope?"

In growing indignation, she heard Dev's cheerful reply. "But of course I am. God forbid that I ever number more than one refractory, contumacious female among my acquaintances."

"By George, that *would* be more than a man could bear."

"Yes. But that fireman—a most admirable character! —plucked Nell off her feet and set her aside when she wouldn't do his bidding. You may be certain I'll take a leaf from *his* book."

And she had foolishly imagined tenderness in his eyes when he wiped the rain off her face, silly wet-goose that she was.

Running down the last few steps, she thrust the chamois pouch at Dev. "Here's twelve pounds. How much more do I owe you?"

Dev turned, his eyes raking her flushed face. A grin tugged at the corners of his mouth as he accepted the purse. "You owe me nothing else."

Nell glared at him. The exasperating man knew that she had overheard his exchange with Cyprian. He knew that he had ruffled her.

She set her lamp on the buhl table before facing him again. "Of course I owe you," she said crossly. "I must have counted close to two dozen firemen, and you paid them a guinea each."

"Thirty firemen. You see," he said apologetically, "it was a rather small engine. Some of the larger ones are manned by forty, fifty, even sixty men."

Nell vouchsafed no reply. She did not doubt he had misunderstood on purpose.

"And a good thing it was," said Cyprian, "that Dev had the necessary blunt on hand. For a moment there, after you went upstairs, it was touch and go whether they'd start the pump after all. Quite on edge they were, muttering about damping the walls in case the fire should rekindle."

"Fustian." Nell refused to admit she had feared just that and had left the entrance hall only because Dev was there to keep an eye on the firemen. She did some quick mental calculations on the expenditure he had incurred on her behalf. The result was staggering.

"I still owe you nineteen pounds and ten shillings," she said, giving Dev a reproachful look. "How could you! Is this your latest scheme, to break me financially so that I must give up the house?"

All warmth was wiped off his face. "That was unworthy of you, Nell, and quite uncalled for."

Her indignation wavered. *Had* she wronged him with her accusation? She'd like to believe she had.

"I'll keep your twelve pounds," he said with icy hauteur. "But the balance is *my* contribution. If there really had been a fire, my part of the house would have been endangered as well."

"Dev—"

He turned and walked toward the back stairs. "Come on, Cyprian. Let's see if Chadwick has left us some of that brandy."

Nell caught up with him before he had taken three steps. Tugging on his sleeve, she said, "Dev, I apologize. I should not have said that."

He stopped and glanced at her, but the expression in his eyes did not soften. "I accept your apology."

"You may be odious and frighten away my pupils," she said, giving him a look, part mischievous, part challenging. "You may try to keep my friends from seeing me, but you are too much of a gentleman to resort to underhanded financial dealings."

A tinge of red crept into his face. He removed her fingers from his sleeve and became absorbed in smoothing the crushed fabric. "I said I'll accept your apology. So don't let it worry you."

"Dashed right!" Cyprian said warmly before brushing past them in the narrow entrance hall and clattering down the kitchen stairs. "Dev wouldn't serve you a backhanded turn. Not even to win his wager."

"Wager!" Her eyes flew to Dev's face, then narrowed. "What is he talking about? What kind of wager do you have with Cyprian that would involve me?"

She was intent on her scrutiny of Dev, who was for once speechless, and she paid little attention to the growing commotion outside her open front door. It was Dev's look and his change of expression from sheepish to relieved that made her turn her head in time to see two women, one dressed in serviceable gray, the other a vision of elegance in a pale blue traveling gown, a matching pelisse and bonnet trimmed with black satin ribands, step cautiously across the sill.

The elegant lady was not in the first blush of youth, but her complexion was as immaculate and glowing as that of a young girl. Her features were appealing with dimpled pink cheeks, a dimpled chin, small nose, and bright, light blue eyes. She was not much taller than Nell, but several pounds plumper.

"Nell, my love!" she exclaimed, raising the hem of her gown lest it touch the wet and dirty tiles of the entrance hall. "What on earth is going on? I had to leave my carriage in Cavendish Square and *walk*. And in a drizzle, too!"

"Bess!" Torn between pleasure and dismay, Nell rushed to embrace her friend. "What a time you chose for your arrival! And complaining about a drizzle when all day long we've suffered one downpour after another."

"Nell, you're *wet*." Bess squealed and struggled out of Nell's arms. "I won't stay in a leaking house, I tell you. Not even for you. I've had enough of that when I was in Portugal with my poor Godfrey."

"I assure you, Bess, there's no lea—"

"And what is this smell?" interrupted the fastidious Mrs. Wainwright, wrinkling her nose. "I've tried to ignore it, but, my dear, it is simply too awful." She looked at Nell, her eyes dancing. "No, don't answer me. You wrote that you have no cook. I daresay you worked in the kitchen yourself and burnt my dinner."

"I have not had a chance to *start* your dinner," Nell said indignantly. "Cyprian—you remember Cyprian Westcott, don't you? He wanted to be clever and used grease to light a fire under an old spit."

"Of course I remember Cyprian. But I don't understand what he's—" Bess blinked, seeming to notice Dev's presence for the first time. "Devil Mackenzie, too," she said, peering at him rather uncertainly. "It is a great pleasure, I'm sure. But ought you to be running tame in Nell's house while she had no chaperon?"

"Just what I've been saying." An engaging twinkle in

his eyes, Dev stepped forward and raised the widow's hand to his lips.

Chapter Twelve

Nell was given no opportunity to deal with Dev's audacious remark in the manner it deserved.

First, Bess's coachman and groom arrived, complaining about the slowness of the fire engine and the reluctance of "gapeseeds and curious wenches" to clear the street. The groom demanded to know whether to unload Mrs. Wainwright's luggage and where to put it.

Then, while the two men huffed and puffed under the weight of Bess's four trunks, which must be hauled up the narrow stairs to the third floor, Cyprian, Hugh, and Wicken emerged from belowstairs arguing fiercely and, Nell thought, pointlessly, about the length of time it would take to rid the house of smoke odors.

She was beginning to feel weary and quite chilled in her clinging, wet gown but comforted herself with the knowledge that the three cork-brained authors of her discomfiture and Dev, who had done his utmost to contribute his mite to her dilemma, must be quite as wet and cold as she was.

Cyprian greeted Bess Wainwright with the casual negligence of a longtime friend. When Nell introduced Hugh Chadwick, however, the major required a nudge from her before he stopped staring at Bess long enough to execute a bow.

"Forgive me," he stammered, his swarthy countenance suffused with red. "I never dreamed—Nell said she was expecting a widow. Surely you're too young—" He broke off, struggling for composure, then added in a rush, "My dear Mrs. Wainwright, you behold me completely bowled over."

Blushing prettily, Bess giggled. "I am two-and-thirty. Not so *very* young."

"A mere fledgling to my forty years," Hugh assured her solemnly.

Nell allowed herself a tiny smirk. Hugh Chadwick, confirmed bachelor, hit by Cupid's arrow at last! What fun she'd have teasing him.

Wishing to share the joke, she turned instinctively to Dev. He was watching her but did not seem to see the laughter in her eyes. Ah, well. She had forgotten that he did not know Hugh as she did.

Besides, the less she shared with Dev, the better off she'd be. It was bad enough that in an unguarded moment she could still feel the touch of his palms against her cheeks, the brush of his thumbs as he wiped the moisture off her face.

She called out to Bess, who was being entertained by Hugh and Cyprian with a humorous if not strictly truthful version of the afternoon's mishap. Bess asked so many questions that Nell had to repeat her friend's name twice before catching her attention.

"Let me take you upstairs, Bess. You'll want to see your room, and I must change into a dry gown."

"What a scatterbrain I am!" All contrition, Bess clasped Nell's hand. "Here you must be catching your death in your wet clothes, and I keep chattering on as though I were at a tea. Up you go, my love," she said, assuming a strict-governess tone. "And let me have no nonsense from you."

Too well acquainted with Bess's quirks and inconsistencies to be disconcerted, Nell replied meekly but with a twinkle in her eyes, "Yes, ma'am. I wouldn't dare disobey you. After all, you're the chaperon."

"We'll be off, too," said Dev, clapping Cyprian on the

back. "Wicken, I expect Miss Nell and Mrs. Wainwright to have dinner with me in an hour. You'll see to it that they don't dawdle, won't you?"

He awaited no one's consent but strode to the door. Over his shoulder he said, "Chadwick, you will join us? You're welcome to anything you may fancy in my wardrobe."

Hugh assented with alacrity, and before Nell could say more than, "I'll be dashed if I let you order me around, Dev!" the gentlemen had departed.

There was nothing to be done but retreat to her room and change. In vain did Nell try to awaken a sense of ill usage in Bess. Her friend found no fault with Dev's suggestion that they join him for dinner. In fact, she believed him to be singularly kind and thoughtful for a gentleman of his reputation.

"Godfrey did not like him," she confessed. "Said he is a brash, devil-may-care here-and-thereian, but I cannot deny that I've always had a soft spot for Dev. So handsome and dashing!"

"So high-and-mighty," muttered Nell when Bess left her to go to her own room where Fletcher, her abigail, waited to help her change.

Nell stripped off her wet gown and reached for an old frock of brown merino she had worn at the Bath academy. It was long-sleeved, high-necked, and perfectly suited to fight shivers and chills. At the last moment, she changed her mind. Since Bess was set on obeying Dev's command, Nell must of necessity accompany her—but she need not give him the satisfaction of seeing her dressed like a frump.

As she slipped a gown of deep amber muslin over her head, she did wonder if some small flaw had warped her logic. Her doubts lasted only until she looked into the mirror, when she cheerfully consigned logic to perdition. The rich color of her gown brought out golden highlights in her tawny hair, and if the neckline was not as low as current fashion demanded, the scalloped edge of her décolletage and the tiny puffed sleeves were vastly becoming. A handsome Indian silk shawl shot with gold completed her toilette.

By the time Bess had exchanged her traveling dress for a dinner gown of pale lavender crepe and set a wisp of frilly lace atop her shining blond curls, Nell was convinced that going to dinner next door was not only sound common sense—*she* had no desire to slave over the stove tonight—but was also setting her above a petty and childish exhibition of defiance.

"I've never changed so quickly," said Bess with a glance at the small clock on her dresser. "And without help. Fletcher is not a good traveler. I sent her to bed." She draped a white cashmere shawl around her shoulders. "Do you suppose the gentlemen are ready for us? Mayhap we should wait awhile before we go."

Nell was concerned more about appearing overeager than the gentlemen's readiness to receive them, but given the choice of sitting in her own smoke-scented parlor or following an inclination to vulgar curiosity, she opted for the latter. Thus it was well within the hour Dev had allotted that Nell and Bess left the house with Wicken accompanying them down the front steps of Number Two-A, a few paces along the flag-walk, and up the opposite steps of Number Two.

The door was opened by a frail, stooped butler who greeted them with a beaming smile and the information that his lordship was expecting them in the drawing room. A footman then took over, ushering Nell and Bess to the first floor, while the butler, with whom Wicken appeared to be on excellent terms, invited the old soldier into the kitchen quarters.

Nell moved as one in a dream. When she had first set foot into her own house, she had thought it sumptuous beyond compare. Of course, she had very soon discovered signs of neglect, had noticed that the carpets were past their prime, that curtains and drapes had faded. And yet, except for the lack of furniture, she had considered Number Two-A an elegant house—until she stepped through the front door of its counterpart.

The only factors her entrance hall and Dev's had in common were the tiled floor and the buhl table against the dividing wall. The paint on her walls was old and faded; Dev's were covered with exquisite Chinese paper. A large gilt-framed mirror hung above his buhl table and several oil lamps high on the walls spread a warm glow even into the deep recess below the staircase.

The wallpaper continued up the stairs, as did the light fixtures. Her feet sank into lush carpeting, and when she turned the corner on the first-floor landing, she was dazzled by crimson and gold decor, by landscapes in massive frames hung between two doors. The footman threw open one of those doors, and Nell stepped into a drawing room of such magnificence that her breath caught in her throat.

She tried to take in every detail at once, beautifully carved chairs with brocade seat and back cushions, bureaus and tables which to her inexperienced eye looked of the French Sun King's period, rugs as lush in color and texture as any she had seen in India. She quite failed to see her host until he stood directly in front of her and her nose was about to bump against the top button of his waistcoat.

"Welcome, Nell. Bess."

His voice, deep and full of laughter—as though he recognized her befuddled state—had a salutary effect on Nell. She shook off the feeling of paralyzing awe. Bestowing a casual nod on Dev, she drew Bess toward the fireplace where Hugh, almost a stranger in his borrowed civilian clothing, and Cyprian stood warming their coattails and their brandy glasses before a crackling fire.

The irony of the scene struck her forcefully: the two men who had rendered her house uninhabitable, smiling at her; behind them dancing flames, warmth—and no smoke.

She sat down in the chair Cyprian had placed solicitously near the fire. Her eyes fell on Dev standing at a marquetry table to her left. He was pouring sherry for her and Bess. The decanter was crystal, as were the glasses.

Nell had seen him pour wine innumerable times, but always into tin or pewter cups, and always in surroundings no different from her own. There had been the officers' quarters in Lisbon, tents and peasant huts on the trek through Portugal and Spain. Now she saw him in his own milieu, and it was as far removed from hers as the sky from the ground.

Dev owned estates in Scotland and would some day be the proud owner of vast properties in England. He was the future Duke of Stanford. But it wasn't merely that Dev was wealthy and a peer. Dev had background. He was an integral part of a very old and respected family. He was a Fenton of Stanford Hall.

While they made small talk and waited for dinner to be announced, Dev identified family portraits at Bess's request. Cyril Akin Fenton, Dev's grandfather, occupied the place of honor above the mantel. The grim-looking old duke was flanked by Dev's father and older brother, who had both perished in an influenza epidemic.

Nell recognized Dev's features in each of the three men, his masterful chin, the chiseled planes of cheeks and forehead, and the finely drawn mouth. But the resemblance ended there. Dev's father and older brother had raven hair and piercing gray eyes, and judging by his black brows, the old duke's hair had very likely been dark before it turned a silvery white. Although his eyes were as deep a blue as Dev's, it was impossible to imagine that a devilish gleam had ever brightened their somber expression.

That air of mischief, his penchant for deviltry, Dev had indubitably inherited from his mother, whose full-length portrait graced the wall opposite the fireplace. The late Marchioness of Ellsworth, nee Miss Fiona Mackenzie, held the same secret laughter in her eyes that Nell had often caught in Dev's, and from her he had inherited his shock of chestnut hair.

Dev was a Fenton and a Mackenzie—part of *two* very old and respected families.

Nell had no immediate family. Her father and mother had been the only offspring born to aging couples. Nell believed there might be a distant cousin or two, but since her parents had maintained contact with England only as long as her grandparents had been alive, she did not know who they were or where they lived.

She was simply Nell Hetherington of no permanent home—until she inherited Number Two-A, Chandos Street.

With thoughts like those to occupy her mind, it was no great wonder that Nell was quiet and withdrawn during the four-course meal. In fact, she barely noticed what she ate. When she caught Bess stifling a yawn during the dessert course, she suggested that they return home immediately.

Bess smiled apologetically. "I don't know why travel should be so fatiguing. I did nothing but sit and doze or glance at a book or the countryside."

"It's the constant motion," said Hugh, pulling back her chair and offering his arm to support the beautiful young widow next door.

Dev exchanged a look with Cyprian, who said immediately, "Ladies, pray accept my apologies for not accompanying you. Allow me to bid you a good night right here in the comfort of the dining room."

Nell had not missed the exchange of looks between the two men and was certain that Dev planned to take advantage of Hugh's preoccupation with Bess. Lombard Street to an eggshell, he would say something outrageous to her as soon as everyone else was out of earshot. She was in no mood, however, to have a peal rung over her for whatever Dev might imagine she had done wrong, or to listen to a renewal of his offer to buy her house.

She frowned at Cyprian. "It would not hurt you to wait a few moments for the port and cigars. In fact, you might enjoy your wine better if you had a bit of exercise first."

Cyprian grimaced, and instantly Bess cried out against Nell. "Don't be cruel, my love. Don't you see his arm is paining him?"

"Bess, he need not walk on his arm."

But Bess swept out, her hand tucked confidingly into the crook of Hugh's elbow. With a last irritated glance at Cyprian, Nell followed.

Dev fell into step beside her. "That was the most garrulous I heard you all night."

"I knew you would say something disagreeable." She whisked around the newel post and started down the stairs just as Hugh opened the front door below and ushered Bess out into the night. "Knew it the moment you conspired to leave Cyprian behind."

Dev gave a low chuckle. "Nell, you are as much of a widgeon as your dear chaperon. I didn't say it to be disagreeable. I am concerned about you. All night you barely uttered three words. *Very* unlike you. I fear you must have caught a chill in the rain."

She shook her head.

"If you're worried about the smell of smoke in your

house, you needn't be. I'll send my housekeeper to you in the morning. Believe me, Mrs. Ingles and her maids are death on soot and ashes.''

She wanted to fob off his solicitude but made the mistake of looking up at him as he walked down the stairs a little behind her. His eyes held a warmth, a depth of caring he did not often show, and he smiled at her in that special way that had first captured her heart.

He still possessed it.

She misjudged her next step, lost her balance, and cried out. Strong fingers bit into her shoulder, an arm clamped around her waist, and the sensation of falling into a void ceased. Then she was crushed against a hard chest.

"How can you be so careless!" Dev scolded in a voice that was oddly unsteady. "Unfit to do anything on your own.''

Breathing deeply to calm her hammering heart, Nell agreed with his verdict of carelessness. The result she feared was not, however, a fall down the stairs but that he might have read her feelings for him in her face.

Dev's crushing embrace tightened as she mumbled something unintelligible into the fabric of his coat. "I had better carry you," he said, suiting action to his words. "Before you break a leg.''

At first she lay stiffly in his arms and hardly dared breathe or glance at him. Not knowing what to do with her hands, she clasped them across her midriff and held her head carefully away from his shoulder.

He carried her down the last few steps, out his front door, then asked if she wished him to vault the railing with her—a question that put an instant stop to her reserve.

"Dev, you're mad!" She pummeled his chest, reconsidered, and grasped his lapels instead. "Put me down this instant!''

"Knew that would get you," he said calmly, as he proceeded down to the flag-walk. "For your information, it is much easier on the gentleman when the lady he carries puts her arms around his neck and does not keep herself as stiff as a board.''

She looked around for Bess and Hugh, but they must

have gone inside. Following Dev's advice, she curled one arm around his neck. "You need not carry me at all."

He merely grinned. Not until he stood inside her foyer did he set her on her feet. "There. Now you should be safe."

"Do you know—" she looked at him curiously. "For one who cannot wait to see the last of me, you show a great deal of concern. You might have let me go hungry tonight or let me fend for myself in that beastly kitchen."

"Ah! But then Bess would have had to starve as well. I did not want that on my conscience. Where, by the way, is your dear chaperon?"

Nell's mouth twitched. "In the parlor with Hugh. Don't you hear them?"

"Very proper, I'm sure." He hesitated, then asked diffidently, "You don't mind?"

"Mind? I think it is hilarious. Hugh has fought off every unattached female who visited relations in India in the hopes of snaring a lonely officer, he has rebuffed wealthy mahratta princesses, and here he is well and truly caught after one glimpse of Bess."

"Has it occurred to you that you might lose your companion?"

"No." Her face took on a mulish look. "But I suppose it is quite likely. Are you thinking I might accept your offer if Bess married Hugh?"

"My offer? Oh! You mean to buy your house."

"That is the only offer you made me."

A gleam lit his eyes. "My dear Nell, I believe I shall withdraw it. I find I'm becoming rather fond of sharing the house with you."

"Devil Mackenzie! What are you talking about? Does it have to do with that stupid wager you have with Cyprian?"

"No, no," he said soothingly. "I'll forfeit on that. You see, I bet him a monkey that I'd have your part of the house before the end of the month. But since I changed my mind—"

"You bet five hundred pounds?" she interrupted, outraged.

"Do you think it too cheap? Console yourself, brat. I offered odds. Twenty-to-one."

And she had believed he'd stopped calling her brat. "Good night," she said icily, turning her back on him. "Thank you for the dinner."

She went upstairs without checking on Bess, and prepared for bed. Conflicting emotions raged in her breast. It was not enough that Dev would lose ten thousand pounds to Cyprian by forfeit. She wanted him to lose because *she* had outwitted him. And she would have, too. Only eight days remained of the month of May. It would have been impossible for Dev to drive her out.

Of course, it would have been better still, if she had thought of closing a bet with Dev herself.

Under the circumstances, she couldn't help but worry about the reason for his change of heart. Why did he want her to stay in the house?

She had not mistaken the warmth in his look. He did have a certain tenderness for her. A suspicion, hideous, frightening and yet exciting, filled her mind. If he had finally observed that she had grown up—and not as an antidote either—could he possibly be looking to her as Josephine's successor?

Around and around her thoughts went until, at last, she pounded her pillow in exasperation. It was of no use whatsoever to fret about Dev's possible motivation. She had much better employ her wits in finding a way to tear her love for him from her heart.

Nell Hetherington in love with Devil Mackenzie. Was there ever anything so stupid?

A short while later, her mind filled with visions of Dev's splendid drawing room and the portraits gracing its walls, she sat bolt upright in her bed and said with something akin to despair in her voice, "*I* don't even own a miniature of my parents."

Chapter Thirteen

True to his word, Dev sent Mrs. Ingles and two maids, armed with mops and buckets to combat the smell of smoke. The Dowager Countess of Lansdowne heard of Nell's plight and dispatched three maids as well as her two stalwart footmen with velvets and brocades to replace any ruined drapes. By the time Marjorie Simms trod up the stairs for her final lesson, the third and second floors smelled pleasantly of beeswax, potpourri, and lemon.

"I shan't stay very long." Marjorie sat down on one of the cane-seated stools in the smaller of the two classrooms. "Markham is coming for me between ten and half-past. He arrived in town last night, and I've asked him to take me to Manton's."

"So you convinced him that you can be trusted with a pistol." Nell chuckled, pleased for her pupil, who had on an earlier occasion bemoaned her fiancé's adamant refusal to allow the purchase of her own little gun. "But, then, I did not doubt that you would."

Marjorie frowned. "Actually, he said he'd make up his mind after he sees me handle a weapon."

"That's no problem, then. When your fiancé comes to fetch you, we'll ask him to join us in the target room."

"I did hope you'd suggest that." Marjorie flashed Nell a smile. "I'm used to your pistols, and while I show off my skills, I'd rather have my formidable instructress present than a number of curious and most likely skeptical gentlemen at the gunsmith shop.''

''Just remember to use one of the Mantons. You still tend to forget that the silver-mounted pistol throws to the left.'' Even as she spoke, Nell's conscience stirred. She had promised Dev not to start target practice before eleven—but these were extraordinary circumstances.

''If you like,'' she added, ''you can buy one of the Mantons. The flood of pupils I envisioned never materialized, and three pistols are a luxury I can ill afford.''

''Pupils! Why didn't I think of it before?'' Marjorie clapped a hand to her forehead. ''I've been wondering how I can show my appreciation. No amount of money will ever repay you for all you've taught me in just two weeks, but Markham and I can invite you to the soiree his cousin is giving tonight.''

Nell's face flamed. ''Miss Simms, you misunderstand. You paid me a very generous fee. I ask no more.''

''No, *you* don't understand. Markham's cousin is Lady Melkinthorpe, the renowned political hostess. You'll meet members of the diplomatic circle at her entertainments. There'll be East India Company families, officials from the Admiralty and the War Office. In short, everybody who might know of someone in need of your services.''

Nell rose, her eyes glowing as untold possibilities unfolded before her.

''And please don't feel offended by the lateness of the invitation. Markham and I did not know until last night that his cousin planned this farewell for him.''

''Miss Simms, you are a jewel.''

''It is settled, then. I'll have Lady Melkinthorpe send a carriage for you. Now, tell me again—'' Marjorie opened a dog-eared diary and held her pencil poised over one of the few blank pages left in the book. ''If I want to ask the cook to use only a very little *garam masala* in the curry, I'll say . . .''

Pacing the room, Nell supplied answers to Marjorie's many questions. They worked for about an hour, then removed to the third floor. Bess Wainwright stepped out of her chamber as Nell and Miss Simms passed by her door and, when she had been introduced to Nell's pupil, decided to join the young ladies in the target room.

"Godfrey tried his best to teach me how to shoot." Bess picked up Nell's small silver-mounted pistol from the top of the chest, where Nell kept her weapons, and toyed with it. "But he gave up. Made me promise I'd never touch his guns."

Nell snatched the pistol from Bess. "I'm not surprised," she said tartly. "Don't you know better than to look into the muzzle? With your finger on the trigger, too."

"Oh." Bess opened her eyes wide at Nell. "Is it loaded?"

"It is not. But you could not know that, could you?"

Nell heard a sound behind her, like someone clearing his throat. Turning her head, she saw a stranger standing in the doorway and behind him, Dev with a most forbidding scowl on his face.

Nell noted the smile Marjorie Simms directed at the stranger, the deepening color in her pupil's cheeks, and drew her own conclusion about the identity of the gentleman with the thick blond hair and a face any sculptor would want to use for a model of the archangel Gabriel.

And Dev was Lucifer, the dark, fallen angel.

He had no reason to look disgruntled, though. No shot had been fired as yet.

"Miss Simms," she said before Marjorie could speak to the gentleman who surely must be Stephen Markham. "Please demonstrate to Mrs. Wainwright how a pistol should be handled."

After one startled glance at Nell, Miss Simms turned from a blushing miss into the competent young lady her instructress had come to admire. She removed one of the Mantons from its case, loaded it with admirable speed and lack of fuss, then took up a position opposite the target range.

Miss Simms cocked the pistol, aimed, and fired.

Bess Wainwright clapped her hands after inspecting the tiny hole in the center of one of the wafers. "Bull's-eye!"

"My compliments." The blond-haired gentleman joined Marjorie at the chest of drawers, where she had begun to clean the pistol and return it to its case. "You have me absolutely convinced, my dear, that you're ready to have your own weapon.''

Nell sensed rather than heard Dev coming to stand by her side. "And who," he said in a low but nevertheless cutting tone, "is the Adonis?"

"Mr. Stephen Markham," Nell replied cooly. "Miss Simms's betrothed. And what, may I ask, were you about when you brought him up here unannounced?"

A feeling of ill-usage washed over Dev. He had stepped out of his house just as a curricle drawn by two splendid grays pulled up in front of Number Two-A. A gentleman of about his own age and height but built on more magnificent proportions had jumped down, tossed the reins to his groom with the order to "walk 'em," then approached Nell's door.

The stranger doffed his hat, displaying thick, wavy blond hair, and bade Dev a good morning before lifting the knocker for several resounding raps.

No soldier this, thought Dev, but without a doubt another of Nell's longtime friends. Perhaps this one, too, called her Kitten.

Dev stood outside his front door, held there by a sudden burst of anger. Every rakish gambler the late Jack Hetherington had called friend, sooner or later, would find his way to Nell's door. And since she had grown up with them as her childhood companions, she would not tell them nay.

The stranger raised his hand to apply himself to the knocker once again. Dev said quickly, his voice thick with annoyance, "Don't bother. Probably no one can hear you. They're all at sixes and sevens this morning."

The gentleman turned. The look he bestowed on Dev conveyed surprise and a hint of hauteur. After a slight pause, he said, "I must see Miss Hetherington. I am—"

"You're an old friend, no doubt," Dev interjected. He swung himself over the low railing. "But I'm an even older friend. I'll take you inside. Planned to look in on her in any case."

He'd had no such intention. After spending the morning on a letter to the Duke of Stanford, explaining why his dutiful grandson could not present himself immediately in Hertford-shire and why Number Two-A was still in the possession of

Augusta's bothersome heir, Dev had promised himself the reward of a brisk ride.

But he couldn't very well leave Nell alone with this fellow. He was too handsome by half, and Bess was no chaperon—witness last night when she had disappeared with Hugh Chadwick.

So he had foregone his ride for Nell's benefit—only to learn that the Adonis was the betrothed of one of her pupils.

Instantly, the resentment he felt toward Markham switched to Nell. It did not help to know that she had not asked for his assistance in dealing with the various males congregating on her doorstep. She *should* have asked.

Nell's voice disrupted his angry reflections. "*I* think," she said with a considering glance at Miss Simms's fiancé, "that he looks more like Gabriel than Adonis."

Dev stared at her. "You had better not say that to Markham. No man," he said with revulsion, "wants to be likened to an angel."

"Really, Dev?"

He mistrusted her wide-eyed look of innocence, but she turned away before he could demand an explanation.

Miss Simms and her betrothed were ready to leave. Markham bowed low over Nell's hand. "I owe you an apology, Miss Hetherington."

"Oh?" said Nell, her eyes dancing. "No doubt you believed me a gull-catcher and my academy nothing but a take-in."

"Nell!" Bess Wainwright looked thoroughly shocked. "Mind your language. Please!"

"Pish-tosh. I daresay Mr. Markham has heard a cant phrase or two in his life."

"I daresay," Dev said facetiously. "But not from a lady."

Stephen Markham raised a brow. "There you're wrong, sir. My fiancée has been known to repeat her brothers' more colorful expressions." He turned to Nell. "Marjorie tells me you're willing to sell one of your Mantons. Since she proved herself such an expert shot, I'd be pleased to purchase the pistol from you."

The transaction was completed to mutual satisfaction,

and Marjorie took her leave, reminding Nell about the soiree. "The carriage will call for you at nine o'clock. And, of course, you must bring Mrs. Wainwright."

Mrs. Wainwright, aflutter with excitement, tripped after Marjorie to learn particulars about the treat in store for her. Nell and Dev were left alone in the target room, which seemed all of a sudden too quiet and too isolated for Nell's comfort. Looking up at Dev, she found herself wishing that Bess were, indeed, more conscious of her duties as a chaperon.

Dev saw uneasiness in the clear gray eyes raised to his face. He had been waiting for this moment of privacy to tell her what a willful, unprincipled baggage she was, but with the departure of Stephen Markham, resentment and anger had fled as well. His lecture could wait. Now he had something more important to do. Something he'd been waiting and wanting to do since the day before, when he'd let opportunity slip through his fingers—twice.

One arm went around Nell's shoulders, one hand cupped her chin, and his mouth captured her lips with swift and practiced ease. He was prepared to exercise his superior strength should Nell take it into her head to struggle, but nothing had prepared him for the ardor with which she responded to his kiss.

He reeled under the impact of her fervent embrace. Her arms locked around his waist. Her mouth was soft and yielding, making his senses swim. There was a moment of awkwardness which must always occur when a man of his size kissed a slip of a girl like Nell, but then she raised herself on tiptoes.

Dev gave himself up to pure pleasure. Nothing could be more enticing than the feel of her slim body pressed against his, nothing more intoxicating than the sweetness of her mouth, the scent of her skin.

He did not want the kiss to end, but the simple fact of life was that a man could not go on kissing a girl without getting carried away. He might be a rake and a careless lover of expensive mistresses, but this, he reminded himself with some difficulty, was Nell—the child he had teased in the Peninsula, the young woman he had vowed to protect from the more raffish of her father's friends.

Reluctantly, he removed his mouth from temptation, and

equally reluctantly, he pried her arms away from his waist. He was breathing heavily and had trouble focusing.

Nell, it appeared, was suffering from similar afflictions. Her eyes had a starry look, and her breasts rose and fell rapidly beneath the thin muslin of her gown. Her mouth, full, red, and partially opened, invited more kisses.

Tugging at his cravat, which surely hadn't been choking him when he tied it earlier in the morning, Dev took a few steps away from Nell. "Devil a bit! You didn't learn to kiss like that at the Bath academy."

Nell gave a start. There was nothing starry in the look she directed at him as she reflected how typical it was of Dev to make her feel like a woman to be cherished and adored one moment and like a gauche adolescent the next. She should have known a kiss meant nothing to him.

Well, neither would she allow it to affect her.

With a shrug and a laugh that to her own ears sounded rather weak, she said, "If that was a compliment, permit me to return it. You didn't perform so badly either. In fact, I quite enjoyed it."

A gleam entered his eyes. "Would you care to try again?"

"Any time." Contrary to her words, Nell retreated before his advance. If only he wouldn't smile. "But don't imagine you'll win the house from me with a paltry kiss or two."

"You forget. I don't want your house any longer."

Flustered, she retreated farther until the pins that kept the targets in place pricked her back. Dev came to a stop directly in front of her. He placed his palms against the paneled wall to either side of her shoulders, imprisoning her.

She raised her chin. "And don't imagine you can seduce me as you did Josephine."

"You tempt me, minx." His eyes narrowed. He looked at her intently, but just as she decided she would not be able to maintain her composure and outstare him, he stepped back.

"But permit me to set the record straight, my dear. I did not seduce Josephine. It was she who cast out lures to me."

"In that case I shall be perfectly safe, shan't I?"

Chapter Fourteen

The moment the words were uttered, Nell would have liked to retract them. Her snub was like a gauntlet flung down, and it was not surprising to see the disconcerting glint deepen in Dev's eyes. Devil Mackenzie, like Nell Hetherington, would always respond to a challenge.

However, he merely grinned, saying, "I want to take you riding. Why don't you go and find Bess. Remind your dear chaperon that she has certain duties to you."

"Riding?" Nell blinked. So that was why he had come to see her. "Bess doesn't have a mount."

"She can ride Pepper's dam, a placid mare by name of Marigold."

Nell could think of no reason to decline, and thus it happened that the sight of Dev, Nell, and Bess, often accompanied by Brigade-Major Chadwick and Captain Westcott, became a familiar one in Hyde Park. Occasionally, Nell caught curious glances directed at her, and she remembered again her suspicion that she was riding the mare Josephine had used before her.

The thought put a slight damper on the pleasure she took in these outings, but never for long. Pepper was a joy to ride, the last days of May were pleasantly warm and sunny, and Dev was on his very best behavior. Nell could not be bothered long by anything that might sink her spirits, which had been high ever since her first ride with Bess and Dev.

That day, she had found Mr. Forsythe waiting for her in the small parlor. The solicitor had learned from Wicken of her misfortune with the furnace. Conscience-stricken, he offered to pay for any damages. It was all his fault. He should have warned her not to use the antiquated ovens or the spit.

Nell declined his offer, but asked on a whim of mischief that the former lease holder of her house be made to pay for a chimney sweep. "All the chimneys are smoking badly, Mr. Forsythe. Surely, the fault cannot be laid at *my* door after barely a month of occupancy."

Mr. Forsythe looked troubled. He agreed, however, to see what he could do, and Nell bade him good-bye, well satisfied at having scored a point over Dev.

Further good fortune awaited her. As a result of her attendance at Lady Melkinthorpe's soiree, she acquired three pupils, young ladies whose marriage by proxy to promising young clerks of the East India Company would take place in little over a month. Stephen Markham had also introduced her to two of Lord Liverpool's aides, who had dropped hints that the government might be interested in employing her services as a linguist.

Life fell into an easy pattern of riding in the early morning, teaching by mid-morning, and performing various domestic chores with Bess in the afternoon. With Bess in the house, Nell had no qualms about giving card parties, and soon it was an established custom for Brigade-Major Hugh Chadwick, Lieutenant Anthony Marple, Ensign Giles Fairfield, and their friends to drop in after dinner for a game of whist or piquet at Number Two-A, Chandos Street.

Lady Lansdowne, an avid whist player, was not above stopping for a rubber or two. Cyprian would attend occasionally, but more frequently he succumbed to the lure of White's and Watier's, where the stakes were much higher than the shilling points offered at Nell's.

Dev, resplendent in dark evening clothes, showed up every night.

Wary of his frequent visits, Nell confronted him on the fifth evening. "Why do you come here so often? I warn you, Dev, I shall not tolerate any meddling. If it is your intention to disrupt the game or to alienate my friends, I shall ask Wicken not to let you in again."

His eyes widened. "Meddle?" he said with such an air of guilelessness that once again she was reminded of Lucifer. "What have I done to deserve such a cutting reception? Did I say anything on the previous nights to offend you or your friends?"

"So far, you behaved amazingly well," she conceded grudgingly.

He laughed. "And thus I intend to continue. I promise you, Nell, I want only to enjoy your company and a quiet game of whist or piquet."

She was still suspicious. "And you need not worry about my reputation. Lady Lansdowne and Bess are chaperon enough for the highest stickler."

"The countess, yes. But Bess?" He forgot his amiable best-of-good-friends role and frowned at her. "If you believe that Bess and Chadwick are playing piquet in that dark corner where they retire every night, you're a dashed sight sillier than I suspected."

Nell bristled. "And you're an insensitive clot. Of course they're not playing cards. They're trying to make the most of the few days left to them before Hugh's leave is up."

"I should have thought it *was* up by now." Dev cast an irritated glance at the dim corner near the fireplace where Hugh and Bess sat side by side on an upholstered couch— no doubt one that he, Dev, had paid for. "Didn't Chadwick say he'd be sailing the end of May? We now have the second of June."

"The Admiralty gave orders for the vessel to lie in Southampton until further notice. Something to do with the special orders Anthony Marple and Giles Fairfield brought over from Lord Wellington." Nell gave Dev a sidelong look and added, not without a certain amount of malice, "I'm afraid you'll have to bear with my friends for a while longer."

He had been watching the couple on the couch. Judging by their heated faces, they were engaged in an ardent if low-voiced discussion of some import. Nell's pointed remark recalled his own purpose to mind.

"As long as he pays court to Bess, I can easily bear with Chadwick." Dev took Nell's hand, raising it to his lips. "Let's not be pulling caps. I want to play piquet with you.

You're the only worthy opponent I've encountered since I last visited my grandfather.''

This was high praise from Dev. Instead of making Nell proud, it served to put her totally on her guard. But for her decision to fill her coffers by gaming with Dev, she might have refused him. She was convinced he was simply trying to charm her. This was his way of dealing with her snub. No female, if Dev had any say in the matter, should ever be safe from Devil Mackenzie. His pride would not allow it.

Despite her cool appraisal of the situation, Nell would have been horrified to know how close to the truth she had come. Her casual dismissal of his powers of seduction had put Dev on his mettle. He must prove to her and to himself that he could enslave her heart. *Then* he would kiss her again and invite her to repeat that she was immune to him.

He pursued his goal with dogged tenacity and single-mindedness of purpose. His way of life underwent a drastic change. No more late, convivial evenings at the clubs; but that was, perhaps, just as well. He must rise betimes if he wished to ride with Nell before her pupils arrived.

No longer did he meet his friends in the Green Room of the Opera House to invite some fair charmer to sup and while away the night. He wouldn't miss Nell's card parties for the most dashing of opera dancers.

Nell was a good whist player. She could easily have fleeced most of the officers who came to her house for a friendly game, but, Dev noted with approbation, she was careful to make up her tables so that the players were evenly matched and none would rise a heavy loser.

Only when she played against him, whist or piquet, did the fire of gambling fever flicker in her eyes, and her game became more reckless. Especially when it was just the two of them playing piquet.

It had not been a lie when he told her she was a worthy opponent. She was sharp and had a head for cards. Playing piquet with Nell was more of a challenge than playing against Cyprian, who was an erratic player and let his mind wander. Still, she was no match for Dev. He might have won two games out of every three had he not allowed her to take a rubber now and again. It was not his objective to win her money.

To his chagrin, his true aim was not achieved as speedily as he envisioned. It had been his experience that young ladies—be they of the *ton* or of the muslin company—were quite susceptible to a smile or a certain look he bestowed on them. Not so Nell. He might fluster her on occasion, but she always made an instant recovery.

When two weeks had passed and Nell still showed none of the signs of a young lady about to succumb to his charm, Dev decided to forego his afternoons at Jackson's Boxing Saloon or at Angelo's Fencing Academy. He'd take Nell driving instead. Lest his intentions waver, he ordered his curricle to be brought around immediately and went out to rap on the door of Number Two-A.

Nell herself came to answer the summons of the knocker.

Taking no time to utter a greeting, Dev said, "I've come to take you driving."

If she was surprised, she did not show it. Her eyes sparkling at the sight of the curricle and his fabulous horses, she took an impetuous step toward him. "How lovely. Will you show me the sights?"

"Again?" He regarded her warily. "We saw St. Paul's and the Tower."

"Hardly." Snatching a straw hat with coquelicot ribbons off the buhl table, she set it carelessly atop her tawny curls. "Let me fetch Bess, and we can be off."

Bess Wainwright was not part of Dev's plan, but he said nothing. He followed Nell into the small parlor where Bess, her nose in one of the latest novels from the lending library, was ensconced in the only comfortable chair, an old wing-backed monstrosity of green plush in the bow window.

"Bess! Do but put away that silly book," Nell demanded. "Dev has invited us to go driving."

Lady Luck was on Dev's side, for Bess declined the treat.

"Count me out," she said with a shudder. "I get frightfully ill on those swaying, high seats."

"Bess, you goose!" Nell twitched the book from her friend's hand and set it down on the windowsill. "It is quite safe, I assure you. Dev is driving his curricle, not the high-perch phaeton."

Bess shook her head. "It makes no odds to me. I drive

in a closed carriage or in a landaulet. Nothing else will do. Besides, I don't see why you would need me. Surely you have a groom, Dev?"

"Dev has a tiger," Nell said quickly. "A young boy who stands on a small platform at the rear of the curricle and hangs on for dear life when Dev turns a corner. Useless as a chaperon, I'd say."

Dev grinned. For once he was quite in charity with Nell's companion. "Mind you, Bess. These words of stricture come from a lady who thinks nothing of living without a chaperon and receiving gentlemen callers in her home.

"But I quite understand if you wish to bow out," he said, turning to Nell. He had perceived a way to get complete privacy with her. Without a blush, he added, "Ben, my tiger, has an abscessed tooth and refuses to have it drawn. Until he changes his mind, he shall not drive with me."

Her eyes flashed. "Bow out? Dev, do you dare call me craven?"

"Never. I merely wanted to offer you a way out if you've no taste for my company."

She had *too much* liking for his company. Nell's pulse raced. Quite vividly, she remembered the outcome of her last *tête-à-tête* with Dev. And she did not even have the excuse that his embrace and his kiss had taken her unawares. Her instant, shameless response was proof-positive that she had been waiting for just such a moment to fling her arms around him and draw him close.

She had expected a repeat of his improper advances, but during the past weeks he had not touched her save to lift her into the saddle or to help her dismount. And a good thing it was, for Nell had not been able to decide whether she should repulse further kisses, or teach him a lesson by kissing him back and then showing him how totally unaffected she was.

Well, she certainly would not be called upon to make a decision if she was never alone with him.

Nudging her straw hat until it rested at a rakish angle above her left ear, Nell swept out the door. "What are you waiting for, Dev? I want to see the Tower. All of it, this time."

Dev took no advantage of the tiger's absence or the convenience of secluded nooks and corners in the Tower, or in other historic edifices they visited on subsequent days. He was charming and attentive, but never stepped out of line.

And every time he smiled at her it became a little more difficult to remember that he was merely out to prove he could seduce her.

At times, Nell did forget. She believed he must enjoy her company just a little to show such warmth, such interest in her slightest wish. She had only to mention that one of the attractions of Astley's Amphitheatre was said to be a horse stepping in time to the minuet, and Dev would procure a box at Astley's that very afternoon.

She voiced an interest in viewing the Mint, which had moved from the Tower into new quarters on Tower Hill, and Dev promptly took her on a tour of inspection.

"Dev, I believe you are a sorcerer." Nell turned a smiling face to him as they left the imposing building and stepped out onto the porch with its Doric gallery and balusters. "I have it on good authority that it is almost impossible to view all of the various departments in the Mint, yet here I've not only been shown the vaults but was also invited to actually operate one of the coining machines."

He clasped her elbow and helped her into the curricle, which he had entrusted into the care of one of the many disabled soldiers loitering in the street. "I wish I were," he said. "A sorcerer."

His voice and look were half rueful, half teasing. A longing swept over her to reach out and touch his hair, to lay her hand against his cheek.

Instead, she gave a little sniff and busied herself with the folds of her gown, arranging them about her feet with more care than was necessary. As they drove back to Chandos Street, she reminded herself that he was Devil Mackenzie, and that she had foolishly issued a challenge to him.

She could hardly think of anything else during the following days. If being thrown into his company was a bittersweet experience, she had none to blame but herself. Soon, unless she behaved like a ninnyhammer and betrayed herself, Dev must acknowledge defeat. He was a proud man. He'd want nothing to do with her then—except to drive her out of London for sure.

To take her mind off such distressing matters, Nell used

the excuse of an invitation from Lady Lansdowne to visit Madame Celeste, the most exclusive of French couturières in Bond Street. Nell purchased a gown she did not really need—and could not afford. But, of a certainty, Dev would be at Lady Lansdowne's rout, which, every year on the tenth of June, marked the official close of the season. Only those families who had not received one of the coveted gilt-edged cards with the Lansdowne crest took the knockers off their front doors and removed to country homes, to the more fashionable spas and seaside resorts, before that date.

Turning in front of a tall cheval glass in one of Madame Celeste's elegant fitting rooms, Nell discarded one gown as too frilly; another was too ruffled; and a third, too spangled. If she were to commit the extravagant folly of purchasing a gown costing upwards of a hundred guineas, she'd, by George, buy one that did not make her look like an overdressed child.

During one of her card parties she had overheard Giles Fairfield and his friends describe in glowing terms some young lady of diminutive proportions and exceptional beauty. They had called her a pocket Venus.

A pocket Venus, that was what Nell wanted to be when she entered Lady Lansdowne's magnificent town house. If Dev was about to acknowledge that he was wasting his attentions on Nell Hetherington, she would make him do so with regret.

The harassed salesgirl, carrying off another confection with too much lace around the neckline, called upon madame herself for advice. Madame Celeste came instantly. A sale at the end of the season was not to be sneezed at. She had any number of gowns on hand, from simple *robes de chambre* to the most elaborate *grande toilettes*, ordered and then rejected by her capricious customers.

After one glance at Nell, the Frenchwoman turned to the fitter. "*Imbécile!* 'ow could you show mademoiselle the gowns made for a beanpole, tall and skinny? For thees lady it must, *naturellement*, be the silver-white seelk."

To Nell, she said, "It ees *grège*, ah, what you call raw seelk, but of such excellent quality that eet looks like silver."

Nell could only agree when the gown had been slipped over her head. At first glance, the heavy material seemed to be totally unadorned. From tiny, pleated off-the-shoulder sleeves and a scrap of a bodice, the straight skirt fell in graceful folds to her ankles. A closer look disclosed a multitude of small pearls sewn to the sleeves and bodice, and in a wide band around the hem of the gown.

Awed, Nell stared at her image in the mirror. A pocket Venus.

Madame Celeste, misunderstanding the long silence, cleared her throat. "You are thinking the gown ees too expensive, mademoiselle? I assure you, the pearls are *imitation*, mother-of-pearl. The gown ees only two 'undred pounds. A bargain, *n'est-ce pas*?"

Nell swallowed and was about to decline when she remembered Dev.

But, no! She must not crown one foolhardy act with another.

Determined to be sensible, she took off the gown. "I am sorry, Madame Celeste, but I'm afraid—"

She had meant to say, "the gown is too expensive." Instead, she took a deep breath and plunged headlong into extravagance. "I fear some of the pearls are loose, madame. Please have the stitches mended and send the dress to Miss Nell Hetherington at Number Two-A, Chandos Street."

Shaken by her own recklessness, Nell looked at Madame Celeste. She felt certain the Frenchwoman knew she had meant to decline for lack of funds.

Madame, however, merely shook out the gown and examined the pearls. "Ah, yes. I see one or two pearls that will need more thread. I will have eet fixed this afternoon, yes? I will send eet to Number Two-A, and the bill," she added with a knowing smile. "The bill, *sans doute*, I will send to the Marquis of Ellsworth at Number Two. *Oui?*"

Chapter Fifteen

Send the bill to the Marquis of Ellsworth!

Nell had no trouble understanding madame's suggestion. According to Mr. Forsythe's clerk, Josephine had lived at Number Two-A for well over a year, long enough for merchants to memorize the address. Thus, when Nell gave the same direction, it was assumed that she was Josephine's successor, her bills to be paid by Dev.

Devil a bit! She should have thought of it sooner. Naturally, the former domicile of a courtesan would carry the stigma of notoriety.

Embarrassment and anger washed over her. Nell knew the temptation of telling Madame Celeste to go ahead and send the account to the marquis. Let him make of it what he would. He deserved to be thrown in a pelter.

On second, more rational thought, she realized that he might already have received some of her bills. And he hadn't said a word to warn her, the wretch.

Wondering what deep game he was playing at, Nell drew on her gloves. She gave Madame Celeste a long, cold look. "I beg your pardon? Pray what does the Marquis of Ellsworth have to do with me? You will kindly send your bill along with my gown to my own address."

"*Pardonnez moi, mademoiselle. Je ne sais pas—*" The Frenchwoman came to a stammering halt, put out of countenance for the first time in her life. *Mon Dieu!* She had almost spoilt a sale. But how was one to know that made-moiselle was not what she seemed?

With difficulty, madame recalled phrases of the English language, which never before had given her such trouble. "I am so sorry, Mees 'etherington!" She held aside the fitting-room curtain, then rushed ahead to open the door for her nettled young customer. "I don't know what to say, made-moiselle, except to beg your pardon. You see—"

"Perhaps," Nell interrupted, "you should follow the advice of an old proverb: the least said, the soonest mended." And with these words she swept out onto the flag-way where, she hoped, a slight breeze would cool her heated face.

Too perturbed to stop and hail a hackney, Nell set off on foot for Chandos Street. She must speak with Dev. Must tell him—

What the dickens *could* she tell him?

She slowed down, hoping that a period of reflection before she reached home would bring counsel, but when she entered her house almost an hour later, she was no closer to an answer than when she had left Madame Celeste's estab-lishment.

It was one thing to suspect and be secretly thrilled that Dev might be thinking of offering her carte blanche; Jack Hetherington's daughter would know how to deal with an improper proposal, if it were made. But it was quite a different matter that every shopkeeper and merchant assumed she was his mistress now. In the eyes of the world and the Marquis of Ellsworth, the daughter of an impecunious officer might be the perfect choice for a light-o'-love—but they had not counted on her pride. She would never be anyone's mistress. Ever.

When the gown arrived in the late afternoon, Nell carried the box straight upstairs and thrust it, unopened, into the farthest corner of her wardrobe, behind the strongbox. Lady Lansdowne's rout was to fall on the following day. She would wear the dress then, but in the meanwhile, she wanted only to forget about the dratted thing.

She was still on her knees, her head and shoulders hidden among dresses and cloaks, when a light tap, followed by the immediate opening of her bedroom door, heralded Bess's entrance and brought Nell scrambling out of the wardrobe.

Bess looked distracted, but she was sufficiently alert to ask, "What on earth are you doing?"

Nell straightened and shook out her skirts. "I—I was looking for my long white gloves."

"Oh. Did you find them, dear?"

"No."

Bess took an agitated turn about the room.

Nell watched her for a minute or two, then flopped down on her bed. "Come and sit with me, Bess." Drawing her feet up, she patted the quilt invitingly. "You had best tell me what is bothering you."

Wringing her hands, Bess paced faster. "I am such a wretched friend to you, it breaks my heart! But he *asked* me, you see." She whirled, facing Nell. "What could I do but accept?"

Nell studied the flushed face, the blond curls more disheveled than usual beneath a becoming cap of pink-and-white lace. "It is Hugh," she said with a sinking heart. "He proposed to you."

"Yes!" Eyes glowing, Bess finally sat down beside Nell. She clasped Nell's hand, pressing it against her cheek. "My love, you can have no notion how horrid it is being a widow! To be obliged to live with my parents again or, worse, with Godfrey's mother. But he was a younger son, you see, and we never bought a home. We thought there'd be time enough when the war is over. But then he was killed, and it was too late."

A troubled frown creased Nell's brow. "Could you not be happy, living here with me in London?"

"Perfectly happy. But it's not the same thing as having a husband, is it? Besides, you will get married, and where would I be then?"

Ignoring the last part of Bess's argument, Nell said, "But are you sure? You disliked campaigning enormously. Heat, dust, then torrents of rain and mud. The uncertainty of finding quarters. And now you're planning to go back to Spain with Hugh?"

"Lud, no!" Looking like a cat who'd found the cream pot, Bess gave a little bounce on the bed. "Hugh has decided to sell out."

Nell was speechless. She had known Hugh Chadwick a

dozen years or more. He had always maintained that he couldn't be satisfied with any life but that of an officer.

A wistful note crept into her voice. "He must love you very much."

"Yes."

"And you? Do you love him?"

"Yes," said Bess, a dreamy smile curving her mouth.

There was nothing else to be said. Nell embraced her friend warmly. "I wish you very happy," she murmured into Bess's shoulder. "Both of you."

"Oh, I am rapturously happy," Bess assured her, then proceeded to describe in detail how she and Hugh would live in Devon, where he owned a good-sized property.

Nell tried in vain to pay attention while Bess talked of cows and clotted cream; of Chadwick Manor, which had stood empty for so long. Dev's image, the wicked glint in his eyes as he asked her if she would care to repeat their kiss, his devilish smile as he said, "You tempt me, minx," when she assured him that he could not seduce her, superimposed itself on the picture of Bess and Hugh in wedded bliss.

She loved Dev, with all his faults and weaknesses, his devil-may-care attitude and his recklessness. But he would never ask Nell Hetherington to marry him.

Every day it was harder to face him with composure, to treat him with a show of indifference. And very soon she'd lose her chaperon. Pride and dignity would be her only weapons against his devastating charm.

And on top of that, the worry about the bills from Messrs. Soames and Sadler, from whom, well over a month ago, she had purchased linens and furniture. She had searched all likely and unlikely places where she might have stashed two inconvenient bills, but, as she suspected, she did not have them.

How on earth could a lady ask a gentleman, particularly one of Dev's caliber, whether he had received her bills and what he had done with them?

"It is agreed then," said Bess, cutting into Nell's thoughts. "You shall visit us when we return from our honeymoon in Ireland."

Nell made no reply. She didn't recall agreeing to anything.

Bess got off the bed, her face wreathed in a smile. "I

feel ever so much better now. I dreaded having to tell you, but Hugh was right. He said you were never one to put up a fuss.''

"No," Nell said slowly. "I don't put up a fuss when presented with the inevitable."

"You're the best of good friends." Bess started for the door. "And don't worry about your gloves, dear. You may have a pair of mine for tomorrow night."

"Thank you."

One fist propped under her chin, Nell looked after her friend, but it wasn't worry about a pair of long white gloves that put a frown on her face.

Lady Lansdowne's rout was to start at nine o'clock. At nine-thirty, Dev and Hugh accompanied the ladies from Number Two-A to the dowager countess's brightly lit residence at the corner of Chandos and Queen Anne streets.

They had decided to walk, which was just as well, since dozens of carriages were already lined up in the street to disgorge their elegant passengers. Watchmen and link-boys especially hired for the occasion directed the coachmen where to take the empty vehicles until they'd be called upon to carry their tired masters and mistresses home.

Nell had thought Lady Melkinthorpe's soiree an impressive affair, but it could not compare to Lady Lansdowne's rout. This, Nell reflected wryly, was overwhelming. She was glad of Dev's arm as she moved up the carpeted steps to the foyer. She felt helpless, even threatened by the sheer number of bodies hemming her in. The teeming crowds in the markets of Bombay and Calcutta were nothing compared to the throng of ladies and gentlemen pressing through the countess's door.

Maids took the ladies' wraps, footmen the gentlemen's cloaks and hats, depositing them in two parlors-cum-cloak-rooms. Nell's turn came to hand over her wrap. Her great moment to render Dev dumbfounded.

When Nell had removed her new gown from its box earlier that evening and slipped it over her head, she once again experienced the heady sense of awe that had prompted her to purchase the silver-white silk. Due to Madame Celeste's expert use of tissue paper, the heavy material was unmarred by wrinkles or creases. Straight and smooth, the skirt fell to Nell's ankles, and above the tiny bodice a satisfactory expanse of bosom tantalized the beholder.

A pearl choker her papa had won from some Indian prince in a game of hazard and presented to his wife for her thirtieth birthday completed Nell's toilette. Staring in the mirror, she had been well satisfied with her appearance. A pocket Venus. Surely Dev would suffer a pang of regret at her unwillingness to succumb to his advances.

And then the disappointment in Lady Lansdowne's foyer when the maid took her wrap. The crowd was too thick, and Dev was too close to catch a glimpse of her. Why, even *she* could not see the tip of her toes if she tried.

Clutching her fan, reticule, and a fold of her skirt in one hand and Dev's arm with the other, Nell allowed herself to be borne upstairs to the first floor. She did not know what had become of Bess and Hugh, but she hoped they were not far behind. All of a sudden, she wasn't sure she wanted to be alone with Dev when the crowds thinned and he would see her in the most splendid gown she had ever owned.

He was unpredictable. Instead of being bowled over by her stunning looks, he might tell her in that odiously starchy manner he employed now and again, to fetch a scrap of lace and cover up her bosom.

She stole a glance at him, but he was not looking her way. A dashing young matron ahead of them kept craning her neck and quizzing him about his absence from some fabulous do on the previous night. Her husband joined in. Apparently, Dev had missed not only the most exciting curricle race across Finchley Common but also a bout between two promising young prize-fighters in Hendon.

While Dev was busy fending off the couple's questions about his own activities during the past few weeks, Nell, praying she wouldn't stumble, dropped her skirt and made use of her fan to cover her décolletage. When Dev finally turned his attention to her, she nodded and replied with perfect ease while he pointed out the card rooms; the salon that had been cleared of furniture and designated for dancing; the supper room; and finally, the two huge drawing rooms connected by an arched doorway, where most of the guests had congregated.

A tall clock between two windows of the first drawing

room showed it was well past ten o'clock, and still Nell had not laid eyes on her hostess. Lady Lansdowne would think she had scorned the invitation.

The slow but steady movement of the crowd carried them through the doorway into the second drawing room. And there, ensconced in a thronelike chair, her two favorite footmen standing at attention behind her, the Dowager Countess of Lansdowne held court.

"There you are, gal," she said with a wheeze and a broad smile as Nell sank into a curtsy. "Quite a crush, this. Ain't it?"

Nell eyed the dowager uncertainly. The old lady sounded pleased as Punch. "I certainly think so, ma'am."

"A 'crush' is high praise, my little innocent," Dev murmured behind her.

Lady Lansdowne raised her lorgnette. "And you brought Ellsworth, I see. Quite a feather in your cap, my dear."

Dev stepped forward to kiss the old lady's pudgy fingers. "It's fear of Grandfather's wrath that brought me," he said, casting a teasing look at Nell. His eyes widened. If it had been anyone else but Dev, it might have been said that he goggled at Nell, but immediately he had his expression under control.

An instant of surprise, and that was that, thought Nell, struggling with disappointment and a healthy dose of irritation. She didn't even know if it was pleasure or disapproval of her gown that made him stare.

Dev turned back to the dowager. "Grandfather remembers when you came out. He still has a soft spot for his first flirt, and he'd never forgive me if I declined your invitation."

"Cyril Akin Fenton," Lady Lansdowne muttered. Her face creased in a reminiscent smile until her currant eyes all but disappeared in the fleshy folds of her cheeks. "Now, there was a rake! But," she said shrewdly, "fear of his displeasure didn't send you to my rout last year. So don't you try cutting your wheedles with me, young man."

"No, ma'am." Dev grinned shamelessly and would have moved on, but the dowager countess detained him.

"You and Nell stay awhile," she said. "I'm tired of shaking hands and greeting people."

The two footmen sprang into action, one of them placing

chairs for Nell and Dev, the other directing the stream of arrivals away from Lady Lansdowne.

"Tell me about Cyril," the dowager countess demanded. "Did he fall into one of his rages when he learned that Augusta bequeathed her house away from the family?"

"I don't doubt it." Dev stopped a passing footman who was balancing a tray of drinks. After serving the ladies with champagne, he helped himself to a glass of Madeira. "Thank goodness I wasn't in Hertfordshire when he first heard the news. He must have been awesome. He was still devilishly foul-tempered when I stopped by a month later on my way to Scotland."

Nell leaned forward, an unconscious act that earned her, or rather her neckline, a glowering look from Dev. She ignored him. "Lady Lansdowne, do you know why Lady Augusta and the duke had a falling out?"

"Yes, of course I do. Didn't Ellsworth tell you?"

"Dev doesn't know," Nell said with satisfaction. "Can you tell me, please?"

"I don't see why not. Can't hurt Augusta any longer, nor the *chevalier*."

"A *chevalier*?" cried Nell. "Oh, I knew it must be a romantic story."

"Knew it was a scandal," said Dev. "It always was, when Augusta was involved."

Nell turned on him. "How can you be so stuffy and straight-laced? You, with your love affairs, your flirtations and dalliances!"

"If you were a properly brought-up young lady you wouldn't know a thing about my love affairs." Crossing his ankles, Dev tipped back in his chair until it rested on two legs. His eyes raked her face, swept lower, and honed in on the swell of her bosom. "And you wouldn't wear a gown fit for a West-End comet."

A flush stained Nell's cheeks. "You're beastly! And I don't give a straw for your opinion."

"Children!" The dowager countess glared at them through her lorgnette. "If you want to hear Augusta's story, you won't quarrel in my house. And you, Ellsworth, mind your manners. A West-End comet, indeed! In my days," she said, quite spoiling the effect of her scold, "we called 'em 'barques of frailty.' "

The two offenders begged pardon, but Nell's flush did not subside, nor did Dev's heated look diminish.

Lady Lansdowne took a sip of champagne, then stared into the glass as though in its sparkling depths she could capture memories of the past. "Augusta," she began softly, "was many years Cyril's junior. They never got along, which, I suppose, may have accounted for her early marriage. She certainly wasn't in love with Fawnhope, and when he died she made no effort to pretend she was an inconsolable widow."

"That's when I knew her well," interjected Dev. "She was newly widowed, beautiful, gay, and, to the horror of the family, she was always flitting off to a ball or a drum. Then, in 1796 or '97, she left for Cornwall, and no one dared breathe her name in Grandfather's hearing."

Lady Lansdowne nodded. "Augusta had met her *chevalier* then—I forget his name. He was a fortune hunter and a gambler, and wickedly handsome. Cyril was livid when he learned of their affair. But Augusta was in love. She planned to marry the *chevalier*. Cyril and family be damned."

"She wouldn't have lost much by damning the family," said Dev. "Except for my grandfather, whose bark is worse than his bite, they're a boring, stiff-rumped lot."

Nell couldn't stop herself. "Just like you." Quickly she turned to the countess and, therefore, missed the expression, half bafflement, half pique, that crossed Dev's face. "So what went wrong with Lady Augusta's plans?" she asked. "Why didn't she marry her *chevalier*?"

"He apparently didn't believe her when she swore she'd wed him in the teeth of her brother's opposition. He stupidly forced a duel on Cyril and was killed."

"And so Augusta blamed Grandfather and had the wall erected," said Dev. "Well, she shouldn't have. Blamed him, I mean. Any man worth his salt would have killed the bounder."

Nell shot him a look of disgust. "*I* think it is very sad, and if I had known about it I would certainly have written to her, telling her how sorry I was."

Dev raised a brow. "You were no more than four or five at the time."

"What is that to the point? I learned to write when I was three."

Dev grinned. Rising, he bowed to Lady Lansdowne. "If you'll excuse me, ma'am, I shall leave Nell to you to bemoan Augusta's sad fate. Mr. Forsythe is beckoning to me. I had better see what he wants."

Nell gave Dev a startled look, blushed, then, compressing her lips, turned back to Lady Lansdowne.

And what, Dev wondered, was that all about? He strolled off toward the marble fireplace stretching across the far wall, where Mr. Forsythe, clad in old-fashioned silk knee breeches and a black velvet frock coat, had propped his bulk against the mantel.

"Hello, Forsythe." Dev bestowed an amicable nod on the older man. "Didn't think a solicitor ever took time off from his stuffy law books. Especially not to attend a stuffy rout."

"Generally speaking, you're right, my lord." Mr. Forsythe raised his glass and took a swallow of the amber liquid. "But Lady Lansdowne is a friend, not merely a client. Besides, she serves an excellent brandy. You should give it a try."

"I shall." Dev positioned himself so that he could see Nell. "But I daresay it wasn't to put me on to the brandy that you called me away from my delightful companions. Hope you're not going to tell me you didn't discharge my small commission?"

"No, no. Rather the opposite, in fact."

Dev had been watching Nell. Why the devil had he told her she looked like a fancy-piece? It had been a bald-faced lie. She looked stunning. Beautiful. A diamond of the first water. He could hardly keep his eyes off her, but at the solicitor's words, he whipped his head around.

"What do you mean, sir, 'the opposite'?"

Running a hand through his grizzled hair, Mr. Forsythe harrumphed. "Well, you see, my lord, there is, so to speak, *another* bill. Miss Hetherington found the chimneys in such sad repair after Mademoiselle Josephine's occupancy of the house that she has requested *you* pay for the services of a sweep.''

Chapter Sixteen

''She did, did she now?'' Dev stared across the crowded room at Nell.

He paid scant attention to Mr. Forsythe's involved explanations of smoking fireplaces, unusable ovens and spits, but wondered what Nell might have had in mind when she made the demand. Strangely, he felt none of the irritation that generally attacked him when Nell did something outrageous, just a vague disquiet that she was still up to her old tricks. Hadn't the last couple of weeks taught her anything? He had been so certain that she had enjoyed his company as much as he enjoyed hers.

He saw Bess Wainwright and Hugh Chadwick join Nell and the dowager countess. Lady Lansdowne said something that made Bess look self-conscious while Hugh preened like a peacock. Then Nell rose to take leave of her hostess.

''Excuse me, sir.'' Without ado, Dev turned his back on the solicitor and strode off to intercept Nell as she walked away with her friends.

Ruthlessly, he pushed his way through knots of gossiping matrons and brandy-swilling gentlemen. He had no strategy in mind, no preconceived notion how to deal with Nell, but he was vaguely aware that it behooved him to tread warily.

He had already committed one faux pas with his derogatory remark about her gown.

But Nell had had her revenge, likening him to his boring, stiff-rumped relations. That had rankled. She had also called him stuffy and straight-laced. The cheek of the girl, when it had been to save *her* groats that he'd had to assume the unlikely role of propriety preacher.

Torn between amusement at her audacity and pique that she saw him in such an unflattering light, he caught up with the trio just outside the drawing room.

"Nell, might I have a word with you, please?"

Looking pointedly away from him, Nell kept walking. Drat the girl. Still in a huff. He'd take her by surprise and disarm her.

"Nell, I've come to beg your pardon."

She stopped. Hugh, with a knowing glance from Nell to Dev, walked on with Bess, but a few steps only. Barely out of earshot, the couple sat down on chairs placed at intervals along the corridor.

Chatter and bursts of laughter emanated from the two drawing rooms, and a muted hum of voices penetrated the partially closed doors of the card rooms. The air of a lively country dance drifted from the spacious salon farther down the hall. The hallway itself was deserted except for footmen dashing past with loaded trays. In fact, he and Nell had more privacy than could be expected at a social gathering.

"You were saying, Dev?"

He looked into her upturned face and read expectancy in her gray eyes, but also a good deal of reserve. Once again he remembered her accusations. Stiff-rumped, was he? Hell, he wouldn't dream of begging her pardon if that were so.

He gave her a winsome smile. "Nell, I apologize most sincerely. My remarks about your gown were totally unjustified. It's a beautiful gown."

Under her unwavering stare, Dev tugged at his cravat. Where the deuce was his glibness, his savoir faire? He had lost count of the number of ladies he had sweet-talked. And yet, now, when for some reason it really mattered, he was as tongue-tied as a stammering, blushing youth.

"You look fine as fivepence, Nell."

"Much obliged."

She dropped her gaze, but not before he had seen the faint light of expectancy snuffed. He was aware that he had failed her. He too was disappointed in his choice of compliment. Fine as fivepence might do for a ten-year-old, but it didn't apply to the sylphlike maiden standing before him.

"Nell, you're beautiful."

"Thank you."

Dash it! She did not believe him.

She opened her fan and studied the fine Japanese brushstrokes on the silken folds. "About Mr. Forsythe, Dev. You spoke with him? Did he—"

"Did he say anything about you?" After the awkward business of apologizing and complimenting, the matter of her strange demand seemed an innocuous topic. "Yes, he did."

Nell opened and shut her fan several times. Dev watched in silence, and finally she looked up with an air of resolution. "I daresay he mentioned the sweep."

"Yes, he did."

Her eyes flashed. "Is that all you can say? 'Yes, he did'! I should have thought you'd have a great deal to say to me on the matter."

"I will pay, of course."

She bristled with suspicion. "Why?"

"Dash it, Nell! You asked me to pay."

"Yes, I did," she said bitterly. "And most likely I played right into your hands."

Dev frowned. He remembered the many occasions when he had verbally sparred with her; the times he had bested her. Tonight he wanted only to be reasonable, to convince her that he truly thought her beautiful and that he had no ulterior motive in wanting to pay for the blasted sweep. But, for some reason, Nell was determined to be difficult. Whatever he said this evening, she took the wrong way—or made some provoking reply.

Well, he wouldn't rise to the bait. He would not ask what the deuce she meant by saying she'd played into his hands.

"Nell, you're adorable when you bristle and flash your pretty eyes at me. But I find you even more enchanting when you smile. Listen,'' he said, at his most persuasive. ''The violinists are striking up a Scottish reel. Forget our differences for tonight. Dance with me, Nell?''

She showed him gleaming white teeth, her smile as bright as it was false. ''You do me too much honor, my lord.''

Her simpering voice grated on his nerves as much as the parody of a smile did. ''Stop it! I have apologized. What more do you want of me?''

For an instant she looked like the old Nell, ready to blurt out what came to her mind, but then she compressed her lips and raised her nose like a dowager about to give a set-down.

''I want to ask you a question, Dev. If I may.''

She sounded as though she'd ask whether he granted her leave or not.

A prickle at the base of his skull and the clammy stroke of perspiration on his forehead put him on the alert. Just so had his body reacted in the Peninsula on his lonely, dangerous missions when he sensed hidden danger.

''I'll answer if I can,'' he said guardedly.

''I am certain that you can. The point is, will you?''

''Devil a bit! Who d'you take me for? Of course I will.''

''Did you, by chance, receive any of my bills in your mail?''

Dev suppressed a groan. He should have taken to his heels or gone into attack the moment he recognized the danger signaled by his sixth sense. Now he must muddle through as best he could, lunkhead that he was.

''Bills?'' Perhaps there was yet a way out. ''What kind of bills?''

Her voice was flat and mocking. ''From a linen-draper, Dev. A furniture warehouse. There might be others that I cannot at present recall, but they all would have my name written on them.''

No way out. It wouldn't hurt, though, to be cautious. ''One or two may have come across my desk.''

He knew her next question was inevitable, and yet he hoped she would not ask. He wished Bess would leave her swain and do what a chaperon was supposed to do: stick close to her charge. He wished Chadwick would get up and challenge his right to a private conversation with Nell. He wished—dammit, he wished he need not answer Nell.

But he must. He'd said he would.

"Did you pay my bills, Dev?"

"Yes."

Nell blanched.

He knew she wasn't the type of female to swoon or have hysterics, but she looked so ill he put out his arms to steady her.

She struck them away. "Don't!" she said sharply. "Don't you ever touch me again. I know exactly what you're about, Devil Mackenzie."

"Nell, for heaven's sake keep your voice down."

"Why? Because I might ruin my reputation? Forget it, Dev. *You* have done that for me."

His temper started to rise. Granted, she had the right to be angry, but this was going too far. And there was Chadwick charging up to them, and Bess too. Now he wished them to the devil.

"Cut line, Nell!" he said in a menacing undertone. "If you don't like it that I paid your bills, you need only reimburse me."

"Indeed!" Nell forestalled any questions or exclamations from Bess with an impatient wave of her hand. Her eyes never left Dev's face. "And how, pray tell, will settling with you convince the shopkeepers that I am *not* your mistress?"

Loud and clear, Nell's voice rang out, echoing down the hallway, in the exact moment that the violinists chose to stop their fiddling. Perspiration soaked Dev's collar. They must get away before the hallway filled with curious gapers and gossipmongers.

He swept Nell into his arms and, despite her valiant struggles, carried her up the stairs to the second floor. He kicked open the first door he saw, stormed into the room dimly lit by a small lamp atop a cluttered desk. None too gently, he set Nell on her feet.

"How dare you!" Her hair was ruffled, and she looked like a kitten ready to unsheathe its claws.

"Pray contain your indignation a moment longer," he said dampeningly. "At least until I've shut the door."

But before he could do so, Bess and Hugh entered at a run.

"Ellsworth!" Hugh raised his fists in a suggestive manner. "You better have a damn good reason for your conduct."

"Nell, has he hurt you?" cried Bess. Without waiting for a reply, she turned on Dev. "You, sir, are a brute!"

Dev glared at them but made no effort to defend himself. No one and nothing would stop him from saying his piece to Nell.

He faced her. "I think you have some explaining to do, young lady. Why the devil should anyone in his right mind take you for my mistress?"

She was still pale, but two spots of color burned high on her cheeks. "Don't enact the insulted gentleman, Dev. That was what you planned, wasn't it?"

Dev fastened his hands on the back of a chair. He mustn't wring her neck. Not before he'd told her what he thought of her. How *could* she believe him capable of planning her ruin!

He opened his mouth to utter a few well-chosen words of condemnation, when, suddenly, and totally against his will, he saw matters from her point of view.

And what he saw was damning. As was the heavy silence between them.

"No!" he shouted.

"Yes," said Nell. "Number Two-A was established as your mistress's domicile when you had the poor taste to settle Josephine in your great-aunt's house. Shopkeepers have long memories. Unfortunately, I was not alerted until Madame Celeste assured me that, *naturellement*, she would send my bill to you."

"Nell—"

"You paid my bills, thereby confirming my improper status."

Dev shook his head, but he couldn't bring himself to drag Mr. Forsythe into the matter. Not at this point.

"You don't protest, Dev?" Nell sent him a mocking glance. She looked at Bess and Hugh, but they stood in shocked silence.

Slowly, Nell started to walk to the door. "And that's not all, Dev," she said quietly as she stepped out into the corridor. She looked at him over her shoulder. "You made sure that I rode Pepper for all the world to see. Josephine's mount.''

Shock registered on his face—all the confirmation she needed.

Nell firmly shut the door. She had rendered Dev dumbfounded after all, but how bitter was the victory.

Her surroundings blurred. Nell gave a defiant little sniff and slowly, holding the banister tightly, made her way down to the party rooms. No doubt she was growing light-headed from lack of food. That was the reason she couldn't see clearly. She'd find the supper room and sit in a corner to nibble on a piece of fruit or cheese. And then she'd go home.

She came to an abrupt halt halfway down the stairs. Number Two-A could be her home no longer.

Her academy was a failure. Well, she amended, if not exactly a failure, three pupils could hardly be termed a success. Bess would marry and leave before she had ever properly started to be a chaperon. And, what was more, she could not bear living next door to Dev. She loved him, fool that she was, and he had done his best to ruin her.

She could have, with a little effort, laughed at his attempts to seduce her. That would have been in private. But he had made his intentions known to the world. That was unforgivable.

Nell swallowed hard. She didn't know what hurt more, that Dev had proven himself a cad or that she would never see him again.

And what the deuce did it matter? she asked herself, dashing the back of her hand across her eyes. One was as bad as the other, and she'd simply have to learn to live with that tight feeling in her chest.

Resolutely, she resumed her descent. Mr. Forsythe must sell the house for her, but it was galling to know that Dev would undoubtedly be the buyer.

Her hand encountered the carved dome of the newel post, signal that she had reached the foot of the stairs. A deep, pleasant, and vaguely familiar voice greeted her cheerfully.

''Miss Hetherington! Finally. I had almost given up finding you in this crush.''

''Excuse me.'' Nell fumbled in her reticule for the

scrap of linen and lace, obligatory accessory to a lady's gar-
derobe. "Something in my eye. Thought I had taken care of
it, but—"

When she had wiped her eyes, she had no trouble recognizing the older of Lord Liverpool's aides, whom she had
met at Lady Melkinthorpe's soiree.

She held out her hand politely. "Sir Nathan. What a
nice surprise."

"Not exactly a surprise." The slender, silver-haired
gentleman bowed over her hand, then tucked it in the crook
of his arm. "Our meeting was planned, you see."

He had her full attention now. "Planned, Sir Nathan?"

"Government business must often be conducted in secrecy. Meeting you here, where, after all, meeting and mingl-
ing are the order, seemed the best way."

"And what sort of business might you have with me?"

"Miss Hetherington, will you trust me and accompany
me downstairs? In one of the back rooms, the butler assured
me, we can be quite undisturbed."

Intrigued, Nell allowed him to guide her to a small
chamber on the ground floor. It was furnished with a comfortable daybed beneath the portrait of a gentleman in a curled
and powdered wig, several chairs, a quantity of bright rugs
and large lamps, and a sewing table placed near enough the
windows and the fireplace to benefit from light as well as
warmth. Obviously Lady Lansdowne's private sitting room.

Nell sat down in a chair by the sewing table and accepted
the glass of champagne Sir Nathan poured for her at a credenza in the shadowy corner by the door.

He smiled at her. "You are not afraid, I hope? Let me
assure you that I have no improper designs on you."

Her breath caught, but almost instantly she relaxed.
Surely, if he knew of her blotted reputation, Sir Nathan would
not refer to it. He was too much of a gentleman to put her
to the blush.

"I am not afraid. You have already told me it is business
you wish to discuss, and I accept your word. But I admit to
overwhelming curiosity. Why the secrecy? Why could you
not have called on me at home?"

Her heart gave a painful lurch. Not her home much
longer.

"Miss Hetherington, I must first have your oath that you will not disclose any part of our discussion to anyone. Will you make that promise?"

"I do."

"Very well. I shall come straight to the point. I am authorized to offer you employment of a most sensitive and secret nature. I had already hinted at Lady Melkinthorpe's soiree that the War Office might require your expertise as a linguist. No doubt you believed you'd be called upon to instruct a few officers in Spanish or Portuguese."

She nodded. That was what she had supposed.

"Just so." Sir Nathan's pale eyes twinkled. "I'm afraid, though, that our offer is a bit more cloak-and-daggerish than that. You see, the men we shall send to you will come under cover of the night. They are already proficient in the language they require, but you will teach them such idioms and inflections as will help them pass as natives of Portugal, Spain, or France."

Teaching spies.

Nell set her glass on the sewing table and gave him a covert look. She did not doubt she could do it. The offer was tempting. And yet, the confrontation with Dev fresh in her mind, Nell was reluctant to commit herself.

"Rest assured, Miss Hetherington, Lord Liverpool will see to it that you won't suffer financial difficulties."

Toying with the drawstring on her reticule, she nodded absently. If only it didn't mean that she'd have to continue living next door to Dev.

Sir Nathan rose. "One more detail before you rejoin the revelries upstairs," he said, apparently taking her nod and her silence for consent. "Tomorrow at noon, send your man—Wicken, I believe?"

"Yes," she said, her eyes widening. Sir Nathan was well informed about her household.

"Send him to pick up a parcel at his sister's chophouse. Make sure you open it when you're alone. It contains thirty thousand pounds."

Nell gasped. "Thirty thousand pounds? What is it for?"

"We want you to purchase Lord Ellsworth's property, which, I understand, is accessible from your cellars. That way, you can teach our men at Number Two without having to venture out into the street at night. At the same time, we can be assured that none of our agents will be surprised by one of your visitors.''

''Buy Dev's—Lord Ellsworth's house?'' Nell stared at Lord Liverpool's aide in astonishment. It was Dev who had wanted to buy *her* part of the house.

But why not the other way around? It might be called poetic justice.

Her eyes aglitter with some unfathomed emotion, Nell jumped to her feet. ''By George! I'll do it.''

Chapter Seventeen

Sir Nathan solemnly shook Nell's hand to seal the bargain. He handed her the glass of champagne she had left untouched on the sewing table, then went to refill his own at the credenza.

''Let us drink a toast, Miss Hetherington. A toast to a young lady—'' He broke off when the door of the small sitting room was suddenly thrust open.

Breathing heavily, his face unusually pale and drawn, Dev towered in the doorway.

Nell's heart leaped into her throat. The sight of him awakened all those raw feelings she had, if not forgotten, at least pushed to the back of her mind during her meeting with Sir Nathan. Misery struggled with anger. She hated herself for the weakness in her knees and the cowardly trembling of her hands that made the champagne slosh over the rim of her glass.

She could not tell whether Dev had seen Sir Nathan at the credenza, but he certainly saw her.

"Nell, you—pesky brat! How dare you leave me to the tender mercies of Bess and Chadwick."

Reproof from *him*. If that didn't beat the Dutch! Her blood boiled. She set her dripping glass on the nearest surface and, in a gesture rivaling the dramatic poses of the great Sarah Siddons, pointed to the door. "Get out!"

Dev kicked the door shut and advanced toward her with a long, purposeful stride. "Not until I've had my say."

She was very much aware of Sir Nathan standing in the dim corner by the door, but the presence of the Prince Regent himself would not have stopped her from speaking her mind. "You are despicable, Dev, and I never want to see you again! I hope Hugh planted you a facer."

"I wish he had!" He leaned close, so close that his ragged breaths stirred tendrils of her hair. "I could have hit back. But it was Bess who boxed my ears."

"Good for her."

Something in her tone or in her eyes must have given away her intent to follow Bess's example. He caught her wrist before she had even half raised her arm.

"Don't tempt me into doing something we'll both regret. Believe me, Nell, I'd be only too glad to put you across my knee."

"You wouldn't dare!"

"Wouldn't I just? I've had the devil of a time getting away from Bess and Chadwick, and when I finally did, it was to make a damned fool of myself searching the whole bloody first floor for you and then to learn that you're enjoying a *tête-à-tête* with some dashed rake!"

"You're drunk. Or mad. Or both!" And she had believed herself in love with him. She must be mad, too.

He gripped her shoulders. "Where is he, Nell? I'll be glad to draw his cork."

"Good evening, Deverell." Unhurried and totally at ease, Sir Nathan strolled across the room. "Haven't seen you since your dear mother's funeral. Hope you're keeping well?"

Dev whirled, his hands dropping off Nell's shoulders. "Sir!" he croaked.

Nell wanted to laugh at the look of incredulity and dismay on Dev's face when he saw the slender, silver-haired gentleman, but she was too angry even to enjoy his discomfiture. With a toss of her head, she resumed her seat by the sewing table. Tomorrow she'd have thirty thousand pounds to buy his house. Tomorrow she'd laugh at him.

"Would you care to join us, Deverell?" Sir Nathan said smoothly. "I was in the midst of proposing a toast when you came in. A toast to a beautiful young lady. A veritable pocket Venus."

A pocket Venus, her mind echoed mockingly. The words she had longed all evening to hear had been uttered—by the wrong man.

"Ah, well." Dev looked hot and uncomfortable. "If you don't mind, sir, I'd like a word in private with Miss Hetherington."

"Surely it can wait," she said coldly.

"It cannot." Dev barely glanced at her before addressing Sir Nathan again. "Sir, I must speak with her now."

Sir Nathan seemed amused. He nodded. "Yes, I quite see that you must. Ever since your precipitate entrance, I've had the distinct feeling that I am *de trop*."

Dev bowed stiffly. "Thank you."

Sir Nathan smiled at Nell. "My dear, no doubt you think me a traitorous old geezer to leave you with this angry young man. But you're a resourceful lady. I have no doubt you know how to use your time with him."

Use her time? That could refer only to her buying Dev's house. But not tonight! She was too agitated and angry. She couldn't think clearly. She wouldn't be able to relish her moment of triumph when she made Dev an offer on his half of the house.

She shot Sir Nathan an irritated look, which glanced off him like an arrow off a suit of armor. A bow to her, a significant wink, and he strolled away, closing the door behind him with delicate care.

Men! she thought with loathing. But rather than sit and listen to more of Dev's reproaches and ludicrous accusations, she'd make the offer and get it over with.

"Dev," she said, giving her chin a belligerent upward tilt. "You must be as conscious as I of the awkwardness of our situation. After tonight, we cannot possibly live as neighbors."

He had started to pace when the door closed behind Sir Nathan, but at Nell's words he spun around. "You don't know what you're talking about. *Nothing* happened tonight, and if you hadn't taken off in such a huff, you'd have known it by now."

Indignation overrode her judgment at his curt tone. She allowed herself to be diverted from her purpose. "Are you denying that you destroyed my reputation?"

"Dash it, Nell! Your reputation probably doesn't have a single stain. Don't you think that I, or Cyprian, or Lady Lansdowne, would have heard if there had been rumors?"

"Madame Celeste—"

"—suggested she'd send her bill to me, I grant you that. But knowing you, you probably told her off in fine style. Am I right?"

"Yes, but—"

"No, 'but.' " He scowled. "She has seen her mistake, and no doubt about it."

"What about the bills you said you paid? Are you denying it now?"

"I gave the money to Mr. Forsythe. *He* paid the merchants in *your* name."

Her eyes narrowed suspiciously. "Why? All you had to do was give them to me."

Dev did not need the prickle at the base of his skull to warn him of dangerous territory. He took a step toward her. "You tell me this, my girl! Why the devil did you take to your heels after accusing me of letting you ride Josephine's mount?"

Nell shot out of her chair. "I did not run away. There was nothing else to say. You should have seen your face!"

"Aye. You had properly floored me. I didn't recover until Bess flew at me. Devil a bit, Nell! I may have been loose-screw enough to install Josephine in Augusta's house, but I'm not so lost to propriety as to let her ride Pepper. My mother's filly."

"Your mother's—" Nell's legs started to tremble. Abruptly she sat down again.

"Mother spent most of her time in Hertfordshire or Scotland," said Dev. "But once in a while she'd be plagued by maternal urges and come haring up to London. First my brother, then I, kept Marigold and Pepper for her."

Nell's mind was spinning. Numbly, she said, "Then she died only recently."

"Just over a year ago."

"I don't know why, but somehow I assumed that she passed away before your father and brother."

"She did not simply *pass away*. She was shot."

"Dev, I am sorry." The pain in his voice touched Nell, but the harsh, forbidding look on his face silenced her.

"Thieves broke into the house one night while I was at my club. Mother woke up and threatened them with my pistols. Unfortunately, one of the robbers was armed as well. I entered the front door just as three shots were fired." A muscle twitched in his jaw. "I was too late for my mother."

Nell sat in stunned silence. She did not ask whether Lady Ellsworth had hit any of the thieves before she died. She hoped so, but it was the memory of her first target practice that preoccupied Nell's mind. Dev had stormed into her house in stocking feet and shirt-sleeves believing that she was attacked. . . .

"I am sorry," she said miserably. "If I had known, I would have warned you about my target room."

He understood instantly. The harshness left his face. "Well now," he drawled. "If I were the cad you so obviously believe me to be, I'd let you go on feeling guilty. But, you see, I realized my error as I charged up your stairs. The intervals between the shots were too dashed regular for anything but a practice shoot."

"Oh." Nell grew warm under his steady look. Gone was his coldness; a smile was lurking once more deep in his eyes. Whatever Dev's faults might be, he did not carry a grudge for long.

"Am I forgiven, Nell?"

The deep voice set her pulse racing. How easy it was to fall under his spell again.

Just a little while ago, she had been miserable. She had

hated him because he hurt her. She had hated him because she loved him, and he was merely playing a game.

She must end the game now . . . while she still remembered the pain.

"Am I, Nell? Am I forgiven?"

She didn't know when he had moved so close to her chair. His leg touched her knee, and the brief pressure of his hand on her shoulder drew a tingling response.

"But of course," she said airily, at the same time shifting her knee a fraction. "Now that I know the truth, there really isn't anything *to* forgive, is there?"

He remembered the paid bills, his vague schemes of using them to get her into his power, and shook his head. "It was a misunderstanding, my dear."

"But it is not a misunderstanding that you're trying to seduce me," she said, forcing her voice into a matter-of-fact tone. "Dev, I have too many important things to do to waste my time flirting. I am sorry I said you couldn't seduce me if you tried, and all that silly stuff. You obviously took me up on it, but, I tell you, it must end."

He stood looking down at her for a moment, then dropped on one knee beside her chair. He unwound her tightly laced fingers. Lifting one hand to his cheek, he said, "Must it, Nell? I was having the best time of my life, and I thought you were enjoying it, too."

Her pulse, barely slowed to normal, started racing again. He *had* enjoyed being with her. He admitted it.

But it was not enough. She must not give in to his blandishments.

Nell had a good deal of resolve. It cost her all of that, and a forceful reminder that even her easygoing Papa had called Dev the most hardened and experienced flirt to cross his path, before she found the strength to snatch away her hand.

"Don't you like being in my company?" he asked.

He looked at her, neither hurt nor resentful, but, she thought, truly at a loss to understand her. It was so easy for him. When he liked a woman, he showed it and took his pleasure with her—until he saw one he liked better.

"I enjoyed your company, all right," she admitted with a grim little smile. She rose and stepped around him to the table where she had set down her glass. Her fingers trembled only very slightly as she picked it up and held it to her lips.

Behind her, Dev chuckled. The sound came from high up. Obviously, he had left his lowly position on the floor.

She drank until not a drop remained in the glass. Dutch courage, wasn't that what alcohol was called? Perhaps it was Dutch comfort. Either way, she could use both. The one to make her offer, the other when Dev was gone.

It was now or never. She must buy the house. Teaching England's spies would be just the thing to take her mind off her foolish love.

Feeling rather light-headed, as much from the effects of a glass of champagne drunk in haste as from a sudden attack of doubts about the daring step she intended to take, she turned to face Dev.

"Yes, I enjoyed your flirting. It was delightful. But now, I am tired of games. I want to settle down, work hard to establish my academy. I want to buy your house, Dev."

"You want *what*?" He stared, then slapped his thigh and gave a shout of laughter. "That's rich! You don't have two groats to rub together, yet you want to buy my house."

"You assume I have no money," she said through stiff lips. "When I told you that Papa left me a legacy, you chose not to believe me."

He narrowed his eyes. "Jack left you money?"

"Yes." It was no lie. Her father had left her one hundred pounds.

"How much?"

"I am willing to pay you thirty thousand pounds," she said, purposely misunderstanding his question. "Five thousand more than you offered me."

He gave a low whistle. "You're serious, aren't you?"

"Never more so in my life."

That was no lie either. She must get away from Dev. Must bury herself in work to forget the love that was tearing her apart.

Why didn't he say anything? She watched him closely, but couldn't begin to guess what he was thinking. His eyes were well hidden beneath drooping lids and lashes.

"Dev, will you sell me your half of the house?"

He shook his head. "The house is not for sale."

"Not—" The words stuck in her throat. He couldn't do this. She must have the house. "Why not?"

His quick grin flashed. "If it's destined to be one combined residence again, it shall be Fenton House, not Hetherington House."

He saw a jumble of emotions chase across her expressive features, some of which puzzled him. Disappointment, even chagrin, he could understand. But fear, perhaps anger? It couldn't possibly mean that much to her. Or could it?

She was up to something. Some madcap scheme. Devil a bit. The girl could get herself into trouble faster than the Prince Regent could think of ways to spend money.

Undoubtedly he'd made a mistake when he decided to let her keep Number Two-A. She was no more fit to look after herself than a newborn babe. Bess Wainwright as chaperon was no great help. If he read the signs correctly, she'd be off with her dashing major before long.

He'd have to look after Nell himself. She hadn't reached majority. He could be her guardian, her protector. Hell, he'd think of something. But first he'd teach her a much-needed lesson.

"Dev, let me speak to—to my banker. Perhaps I can raise the amount."

Her *banker*. He bit down a chuckle. Her banker would have a spasm when he learned that she had bid thirty thousand pounds for a house that wasn't worth twenty.

"I will not sell. But I'll play you for it, Nell."

Her eyes widened. "Play?"

"Piquet. Best of three games wins."

Hope surged. She could do it. She could win.

But dare she stake the government's money?

"Your half against my half of the house," said Dev.

Her breath caught. She reached out blindly, searching for something solid to clasp and hold on to. But there was nothing—save for Dev's preposterous offer, and she mustn't clasp at that.

"No," she choked out. "I cannot stake my house."

He seemed to have expected her refusal, for he nodded, saying, "My apologies, Nell. I shouldn't have made the suggestion. Knew you wouldn't have the stomach for it."

"It's not that!" she cried, stung. He must see that it

wasn't merely her home she'd be staking, but her whole future.

He patted her shoulder. "Forget it, Nell. Shall we rejoin the company upstairs?"

"Don't act so dashed patronizing!"

She shook off his hand, her mind spinning crazily. He'd walk off as though nothing had happened. And tomorrow and every day thereafter he'd still be living next door to her, asking her to ride or drive with him. And, because she loved him so much, she would die a little bit each day, while he enjoyed his seduction game.

He was watching her, a speculative gleam in his eyes. "There was a time," he said with deliberate provocation, "when you would not have refused a dare."

"That's right." She held his gaze defiantly. No longer would she fight the inevitable. "And neither will I refuse now. I'll play you, Dev."

Chapter Eighteen

After an infinitesimal pause, Dev said, "Done. But we cannot play upstairs. The card rooms are crowded."

"We'll play at my house." With steady hands, she picked up her reticule and fan. "Shall we go?"

He opened the door and ushered her into the hallway, then, with a muttered excuse, dashed back into the sitting room. Two full bottles of champagne sat on the credenza, their corks loosely plugged into the necks. Dev cradled the bottles in his arm and returned, a grin lifting one corner of his mouth. "'Twould be a shame if it went to waste."

She made no reply, and Dev didn't press for one. The footmen in the foyer sprang to attention. Dev received his hat, and a maid hurried out of the second cloakroom with Nell's wrap.

They stepped outside. The night was damp and misty. The dull echo of their footsteps on the flag-way and the muffled sound of a carriage rattling over the cobbles in Cavendish Square were the only sounds to break the heavy silence between them.

Dev threw a covert look at Nell, but he could not distinguish her expression in the dim street-lighting. He had quite deliberately taunted her, for he knew that the hardest thing for Nell was to refuse a dare or a challenge. But he also knew how much the house in Chandos Street meant to her. He had expected her to stay firm, to explain why she suddenly wanted the other half as well.

Her quick capitulation had taken him by surprise, and he still did not know why she was set on owning both halves of the house. It was all quite maddening, especially the niggling thought at the back of his mind, doubting the wisdom of his challenge.

Dash it! He knew how to handle Nell. Always had.

And then he remembered Sir Nathan. Nell and Sir Nathan in Lady Lansdowne's private sitting room. . . .

The presence of the familiar, silver-haired gentleman had given him a jolt, but he had been too preoccupied with his own affairs to wonder about the touch of incongruity in the situation. Sir Nathan Welby did not usually spend time drinking champagne with young ladies. He was too busy scheming for the War Office and adoring Lady Welby, nee Mary McLeod, first cousin to Fiona Mackenzie—Dev's mother.

Sir Nathan had apologized to Nell for leaving her and added the assurance that she was a resourceful young lady who would know how to use her time with him, Dev.

And Nell had looked self-conscious, then offered to buy his half of the house.

Having reached this point, it was but a short step to the assumption that the thirty thousand pounds had come from the War Office. Lord Liverpool and his henchman Sir Nathan would snatch at the chance to have Nell with her proficiency in languages on the payroll.

So, she was indeed embarked on a madcap scheme, he thought, feeling a certain amount of grim satisfaction tinged with unease. But it must not be. A young, unprotected girl caught in the web of the War Office—he couldn't let it happen.

But, then, if she lost her house in London, Sir Nathan would have to look for a new candidate, wouldn't he?

Still without exchanging a word, they entered Number Two-A. Nell picked up a lamp Wicken had left burning in the foyer and, barely giving Dev time to deposit his hat on the buhl table, nudged him into the small parlor on the ground floor.

Tugging off her long gloves, she directed him to a cupboard with glass doors and several drawers. "You'll find cards in the top left-hand drawer."

"And glasses?" He set the champagne bottles on the mantel.

"I don't drink while I play." She swept several ladies' journals and books off a table, then lit a tarnished candelabrum. "Have you found the cards yet?"

"I have." He had also found a set of mismatched port glasses behind one of the doors. He tossed her an unbroken deck of cards, carried two of the glasses to the mantel, and poured.

She was expertly shuffling the cards when he turned to take the glasses to the table. Candlelight bathed her bare shoulders and arms. Her face was partially shadowed, her eyes dark and secretive, her mouth lushly enticing. All of a sudden, she was a stranger. An enchantress.

"It is obligatory to have a glass at your elbow when you engage in serious playing," he said, with some difficulty taking his mind off the wayward thoughts she had evoked.

She was momentarily diverted from shuffling. "Is that what you do at White's and Watier's? You gamble and drink at the same time?" A small crease appeared between her brows. "But Papa always said—"

" 'You need a clear head to play cards,' " Dev interrupted. He took his seat opposite her. "Quite right. But Jack also said, 'You can't play when you're distracted by a dry throat.' " . . . *or by a beautiful woman*.

She nodded. 'Twas indeed one of Papa's sayings, but she wouldn't put it past Dev to use Jack Hetherington to get her bosky. "Shall we cut?"

"One moment, Nell. Are you sure you wish to go through with this?"

Her eyes seemed to turn even darker, more secretive. "But of course."

He held her gaze, wondering what she was thinking. Did she seriously believe she could defeat him at piquet?

Nell tapped the cards. "Shall we cut for the deal?"

"Very well."

Nell won the deal, and they settled down to the first game. Except for the obligatory calls, no sound broke their concentration. The game went to Dev in six quick hands, but his score wasn't high enough to alarm Nell. She won the second game, twice scoring a *repique* and once a *capot*, which gave her a fair lead over Dev.

The moment she sat down to play, she had concentrated only on the cards. She had allowed no thought of the stake to distract her, but as she dealt the first hand of the third and last game, the knowledge that she was playing for the very roof over her head could no longer be denied. Her fingers felt clammy and, as she fanned out the remaining eight cards on the table between her and Dev, she noticed that they shook just a little.

Dev picked up his cards. He hardly seemed to look at them before he made his discard. "Four only. Do take a breath, Nell, and perhaps a sip of champagne. I promise you, one sip won't render you cast-away."

He made his suggestion in the same low-key voice he used to make his calls, and it took a moment before she responded. Her eyes flew to his face. "Do I look as sick as I feel? And I thought," she said with a forced smile, "that I was a born gamester."

He leaned back in his chair. "Dash it, Nell! We're not playing for chicken-stakes. If I started to think about what my grandfather would say if I lost the house, I'd be shaking like a blancmange."

"Yes," she said, remembering the portrait of the

grim old duke in Dev's drawing room. "I think I would, too."

Strangely, knowing that Dev—even if he had exaggerated—was not quite as cool as he looked, helped her relax. She drank a small sip of champagne, made her discard, and picked up the remaining four cards on the table. By the time she had scored a *tierce* and a *quinte*, her mind was totally on the game. She had a good hand, and she knew she could play it well.

Noting her absorption, Dev smiled a crooked little smile. Poor Nell. She had not noticed that he had allowed her to win the three hands of the second game that had given her the high points.

This game, the final game, would be his, and he would beat her score.

He won the first hand and had taken two tricks of the second, when his mind started a train of thought quite independent of the game. If Nell lost, she must give up her scheme of living in London. She'd go back to Bath or some equally dull place. She'd be gone from his life, as lost to him as Number Two-A was lost to her.

He looked up from his cards as Nell took the last trick of the second deal. Her eyes met his, and in that brief moment of contact he realized that he did not want Nell to leave London. He did not even want her to move out of Number Two-A. He wanted her where he could see her every day. He wanted her . . .

Devil a bit! Could he be in love? In love with Nell?

His insides knotted into a hard, cold lump at the thought of losing her. And he would, if he won the game.

He did not want to win. And yet, if he lost, *he* would be the one who must move out. A devilish tangle! But he'd think of something. The main thing was to let her win.

He watched her deal, his mind in uproar, his peace cut up. Sharply, he called himself to order. Time enough when the game was played to explore that awesome emotion he had discovered within himself. An emotion that excited him more than winning a game of chance, and intimidated him more than his grandfather's probable reaction to the loss of the second half of Fane House.

He played with renewed concentration, but this time to

defeat his own cards. Nell must win this last game, or, at least, lose it with such a small margin that the second game, *her* game, would be the winning one.

He was leading ninety-eight to ninety-five when he dealt the last hand. Nell would have the opening lead. If at all possible, he'd let her have *capot*.

Perspiration blotted his forehead and burned his eyes. Never before had it been so dashed tricky to let her pick up extra points. Once or twice, he felt her eyes on him, probing, questioning. All-in-all, though, he didn't do too badly.

Nell took the last trick. "*Capot!* I won!"

Her unladylike shriek—ungentlemanly, too, in view of the strict code of ethics that reigned at the gaming tables of the clubs—evoked only a slight wince from Dev.

He *must* be in love.

"I am sorry, Dev." Candlelight reflected in her eyes and, possibly, accounted for the bright glow that contradicted her words. "I shouldn't have shrieked. It'll bring Wicken down on our heads, and he'll scold us dreadfully."

"And I thought you were going to say you're sorry I lost."

"I am." She blanched, as though a very painful thought had occurred to her. Then she raised her chin in the familiar gesture he had come to recognize as a signal of contrariness. "But not very. What'll you do now, Dev?"

"Open Stanford House in Grosvenor Square, I suppose." He shrugged, watching her, wondering why it had taken him so long to see that he loved her. It explained so much. He had spoken nothing but the truth when he told her that the past few weeks had been the best of his life.

Slowness of decision and laggardness in action did not number among Dev's faults. While Nell sipped her champagne, Dev made up his mind. Nell did not need a guardian. She needed a husband.

"Nell—"

Her eyes widened when he thrust back his chair, toppling it. He crossed the short distance to her side. As he had done earlier in Lady Lansdowne's sitting room, he dropped to one knee and possessed himself of her hand.

"Nell, will you marry me?"

Shock, incredulity, then anger, were mirrored on her

face. Snatching her hand out of his grip, she jumped to her feet. Her chair would have followed the fate of Dev's had it not crashed into a what-not and come to a precarious halt on two legs.

"If you think I'll m-marry you just so you can get your s-stupid house back!"

Dev got up. "Nell, please don't cry."

"I'm not crying!" She dashed the back of her hand across her face. "I'm so mad I could scratch your eyes out."

"I thought you might like us to be married." He took a tentative step toward her. "There was a time when you seemed quite fond of me."

"Fond of you!" she shrieked. "When all you do is scold me and tell me what I can and cannot do? When you leave it up to Sir Nathan to tell me that I look like a pocket Venus?"

Dev stared, dumbfounded. Such passion. Such fury . . . like a woman scorned.

He remembered her youthful infatuation with him in the Peninsula. Then, in London, there had been small incidents, confrontations with Nell, that had baffled him—but did no longer.

He had been a numbskull, a lunkhead, and worse. A gleam lit his eyes. He went to her, sure of himself and his victory. He reached out for her. "Nell, my little love. Let me tell you how I see you. You're more than a mere pocket Venus. You are—"

"I am *not* your little love. And don't you touch me, Dev! Unless you want a box on your ears that'll make Bess's seem like a caress."

Dev smiled. He easily caught her upraised hand. His other arm went around her waist. He bent his head to claim her mouth.

The door crashed open and Wicken stomped in. "An' what might ye be about, Lieutenant?"

Dev looked up, his grip slackening. The next moment his head snapped back as a resounding slap connected with the side of his face.

"Get out!" Nell said furiously.

He chuckled appreciatively. "Vixen."

Rubbing his cheek, he considered his options. He had

no doubt he could make Nell see reason. Devil a bit! He must, if he wanted her to marry him.

But, perhaps, he had better explain the situation to Wicken first—without Nell around. The old soldier looked as though he were ready to take a shotgun and pickle him in lead if he so much as made a wrong move. And yet—it was hardly desirable to leave Nell in her present state of outraged dignity.

The opening of the front door and Bess Wainwright's voice precipitated his decision. "Nell, my love," he said hastily. "I shall call on you tomorrow."

Her eyes flashed. "I shan't be at home to you."

Dev bowed, gave Wicken a hard stare, and strolled off. His casual exit was marred somewhat by the tempestuous entrance of Bess, with Chadwick hard on her heels. Dev had to sidestep quickly if he didn't want to be knocked over by the widow. With a sigh of relief, he gained the dim hallway just as Bess demanded to know what Devil Mackenzie was doing in the parlor with Nell.

He picked up his hat, but did not leave, listening unashamedly for Nell's reply.

"We played piquet, and I won his house."

Silence greeted Nell's rather defiant response.

Dev was about to press the hat on his unruly hair, when an idea occurred to him. He put it back on the table and left quickly.

Wicken would know what to make of the forgotten piece of headgear. He'd be waiting after Nell had gone to bed to hear the "lieutenant's" explanation.

Dev let himself into his own house or, rather, Nell's latest acquisition. Light spilling into the hallway from the open door of his study warned him that Cyprian was still up, undoubtedly to tease him about attending the rout. With a look of resignation on his face, Dev entered the study.

Cyprian, no longer wearing a sling, sat in front of Dev's desk, rolling dice, left hand against right. A decanter and two glasses of cognac stood at his elbow, one almost empty. Without looking up, he said, "Past two o'clock. Fairfield bet me you wouldn't make it past midnight."

"He won. I left about eleven-thirty." Picking up the

fuller of the two glasses, Dev slumped into the deep chair behind the desk.

"That's my cognac, I'll have you know. You're a fine host, taking your guest's drink."

"A fine guest, drinking from two glasses at once." Dev downed the cognac in one gulp. He needed it. What with the game, his earth-shattering discovery of love, and the misfired proposal of marriage, he hadn't even had the benefit of the champagne he'd filched from Lansdowne House.

Cyprian pushed aside the dice. He reached for the decanter and refilled Dev's glass.

Again Dev downed the contents.

"That dull, eh?" Cyprian asked with a smug grin. "Don't say I didn't warn you."

"Dull?" Dev considered for a moment, then chuckled. "No, my friend. I haven't had a dull moment since I left the house at eight-thirty."

"Must have been Nell, then. Up to her tricks again, was she?"

She had, indeed, been up to her tricks, and Dev was beginning to understand why. Not only had she wanted his half of the house for Sir Nathan's purposes—and now that Dev thought about it, he wouldn't be at all surprised if Sir Nathan had known how things stood between him and Nell. But the wily old fox wanted to hedge his bets. He'd get the house by hook or by crook, through purchase or marriage. A house, with one half an innocent Academy for Young Brides, and the other half, connected by a cellar door, to be used for the War Department's nefarious purposes. And Nell had agreed to the scheme because she needed the funds— and because it would put the rakish Devil Mackenzie, for whom she had a definite *tendre*, but whom she did not trust, at a safe distance.

Pouring a third drink, Dev stared into the swirling amber liquid. "In candlelight, Nell's hair is the color of cognac."

"I say, Dev!" Cyprian narrowed his eyes. "If you left the rout at eleven-thirty, where did you go? Dash it! Didn't get Nell into a scrape, did you?"

Once more Dev downed his drink. "I'm going to marry Nell."

Cyprian gave a snort. "What a slow-top you are. I've known *that* since I first saw you with her. Question is, will she have you?"

"She will. If I have to carry her off."

"You can't be serious." Cyprian tossed off his own drink. "Are you? Now see here, Dev—"

"Don't talk, Cyprian. I must think."

Cyprian obligingly fell silent while Dev, hands folded behind his head, stared at the intricate plaster-work on the ceiling.

There must be a way to convince Nell that he loved her, that he thought her more desirable than a pocket Venus, that he was not the dull, prosy stick she believed him, but a dashing, passionate, romantic lover. . . .

Two hours and several carefully laid and discarded schemes later, Dev entered his bedroom. He opened the top drawer of his dresser, reached inside, and pulled out a large brass key.

Chapter Nineteen

Nell awoke suddenly. She lay quite still, listening. She heard the pounding of her heart, her own breathing, but nothing else.

Yet something, some slight noise, the creaking of a board perhaps, had awakened her.

Carefully, she eased herself into a sitting position, at the same time feeling under her pillow for the small silver-mounted pistol. But the pistol was in the target room, where she had kept it since the arrival of her first pupil, Marjorie.

Perspiration blotted her forehead. She was not prone to nightmares or fanciful flights of imagination. She *knew* someone was in her bedroom. She *felt* it. She was sure she heard a second person breathing, heard the whisper of some heavy cloth dragging along the floorboards.

Straining her eyes to pierce the dark and gripping her sheets ready to fling them off, she tensed her muscles. She'd jump. Now!

Her feet hit the floor with a thud. Straightening, she made a run for the bedroom door—only to crash full tilt into a hard-muscled chest. Folds of a blanket or a cloak wrapped around her, enveloping her from head to toe, and before she could even think of screaming or struggling, she was plucked off her feet and tossed over a shoulder like a sack of grain.

When her abductor started to move, she screamed. She kicked, pounded with her fists; but her screams were muffled by cloth and a broad back; her arms and hands were shrouded in that same blanket or cloak that covered her face, and he held her legs in a viselike grip. Her struggles were futile, but she would not admit that she was helpless.

The man's movements became jerkier, and she knew they were going downstairs. She squiggled harder, earning herself a slap on the bottom.

"Dammit, Nell!" her abductor said with a growl. "Why can't you swoon like any properly reared young lady? If you keep squirming, we'll both take a topple."

Dev.

No threat of violence could have stilled her struggles as promptly as the sound of his voice. If her head hadn't been spinning from its upside-down position, it certainly would have started now.

He was mad. A lunatic. He couldn't possibly believe she'd return the house if he held her captive.

When they reached the ground floor and still continued downward, she thought she knew where he was taking her. He planned to lock her into his cellar. With the spiders, the mice, and the rats.

She shivered but made no attempt to fight him. The cellar

steps were hard and slippery. Not that she'd mind if he broke *his* neck, but she had a better regard for her own.

She heard the heavy door creak open—it had to be the connecting door, for all others had been greased at the hinges.

And Josephine must have given him two keys. But he had turned in only one, the double-dealing knave.

Instead of setting her down, as she had assumed he would, Dev kept walking. They went up one flight of stairs, and suddenly cool air hit her bare feet.

"Put me down!" she screamed into the muffling folds, but, of course, he paid no heed.

Still they went on. Another door creaked, and she remembered that Dev had a gate in his garden leading into the mews. Moments later, she heard the snorting and stamping of several horses. She was dumped unceremoniously onto something hard and wooden. A whip cracked. The sudden motion, the clatter and rumble of wheels told its own tale.

She forced herself to lie quite still. If Dev was abducting her in a coach, it could mean only that he planned to carry his seduction scheme through to the bitter end. He was mad, indeed. And if he ended up on the gallows, it was no more than he deserved.

"Nell! Nell, my love. Did you get hurt?"

Faintly, she heard his voice. How dare he call her "his love"!

She felt his hands tugging and pulling on the folds of her shroud. About time, too. It was not pleasant to breathe with something scratchy and wooly pressing against her nostrils.

"Nell, speak to me!"

So he was worried, was he? Well, she'd pretend she had fainted—perish the thought—and when she was completely free, *she'd kill him*.

But when she was free, he picked her up so gently, murmuring endearments while he laid her onto the upholstered seat, that she decided it couldn't hurt to hoax him just a few moments longer.

The murmur ceased, but not the caress of his finger against her temple and cheek.

"Nell," he said suddenly, his voice unsteady with suppressed laughter. "You're shamming it."

Her eyes flew open. She shot up, knocking her head against his chin, for he had been bending over her and hadn't moved fast enough to avoid a collision.

She glared at him, her face burning from embarrassment and prolonged contact with the heavy woolen cloak which, she now saw, had covered her. "How was I to know you'd be daft enough to light a lantern in the carriage. Don't kidnappers work in the dark?"

He had the grace to look abashed. He sat down beside her, first pushing her legs off the seat. Her face stung anew as she realized that she was clad in nothing but her nightgown. It did cover more of her than the silver-white gown from Madame Celeste, but it was such an *intimate* garment.

He made no move to touch her, and for that she was grateful. The rattling pace of the carriage made sitting up difficult enough without being thrown off balance by a caress or an embrace.

But how she wanted the touch of his hands, his kisses. Her longing for him was a physical pain. She loved him, the blackguard. And now he was trying to kill both her love and respect for him.

Well, she wouldn't let him.

Covertly, she searched the coach for some kind of weapon. Devil Mackenzie would find out that she was not one to submit tamely to an abduction. Her eyes alit on two leather holsters hanging from a hook on the carriage wall to her right, just beside the lantern. Pistols. Larger than she had ever handled, but probably a more effective threat than her own little silver-mounted gun.

"Nell, did you hear me?" His voice, showing a trace of impatience beneath the coaxing tone, brought her attention back to Dev.

"I'm sorry. I wasn't attending."

"Devil a bit. Here I'm trying to make love to you, and you're *not attending*. What a settler!"

"Save your lovemaking for those that wish it." *Are the pistols too high, or can I reach them if I jump?* "You need not think that merely because you kidnapped me, I shall become your light-o'-love."

He made a sound, half choke, half laughter. "What do

you know of lights-o'-love? But, listen, Nell. This need not be a kidnapping. I was hoping that after I've told you how I feel, you'd come with me of your own free will.''

She did not bother to answer. There was nary a chance of her becoming his mistress, and he ought to know it.

The carriage made a sharp turn. They were both thrown to the left. Nell saw her opportunity to save herself. She scrambled off the seat, lunged for one of the pistols. The wooden grip felt wide and awkward in her hand, but she whirled to face Dev.

Using both hands, she held the weapon steady. ''Tell the coachman to stop.''

He turned a little pale. A muscle twitched in his cheek, but his voice was calm. ''Easy, Nell. The gun is cocked and—''

A sudden jolt threw Nell against the carriage door behind her. She tried not to jerk the trigger. Alas! A deafening explosion and the acrid fumes of gun powder filled the narrow confines of the coach. A second jolt tumbled her sideways onto the seat.

I didn't mean it! I didn't mean to hurt him. Or kill him!

She wanted to look at Dev, wanted to assure herself that he was all right, but for a few moments, while the carriage raced on at breakneck speed, all she could do was cling to the bench for dear life. And pray.

Finally the coach slowed, then came to a halt.

''Dev?''

He was slumped into the corner of the seat, a blood-stained hand pressed against his left arm.

She slid off the bench and knelt by his side. Her hands and voice shook. ''I shot you.''

''So you did. Just wish your aim had been as bad as that first night you shot at me,'' he said, giving her a lopsided grin. ''It's about time I took you in hand. You're dashed careless, my girl.''

She was still quite stunned, as much from relief that Dev was not dead as from her earlier fright that he might be, when she received yet another shock. The carriage door beside Dev opened, and Wicken peered anxiously inside.

He cast one look at Dev, then turned a stern eye on Nell.

"And haven't I warned ye about that temper of yours? Now see what ye done, Miss Nell. And you goin' to be a duchess an' all."

"Wicken! You're in league with him."

The old soldier shook his head at her, much as he had done when she had been a naughty child. "Better tie up the lieutenant's wound," he admonished. "Use his cravat."

"He isn't a lieutenant any more." Her protest was mechanical. She was already helping Dev remove his coat.

"It's nothing but a scratch," he said, disclosing an angry-looking gash beneath the torn shirt sleeve where the bullet had grazed him before burying itself in the paneling of the carriage. "Wicken, I think you had better return to the horses. They've had quite a fright."

"Aye, but they be tuckered out now and docile. They didn't think ole one-arm here could handle 'em. But I did."

"You certainly did," said Dev. "Now, if only you'd believe that I can handle Miss Nell—"

Showing his gap-toothed grin, Wicken slammed the door shut.

Nell snatched the cravat off Dev's neck. Tight-lipped, she set about bandaging his arm, and by the time the carriage started to roll again, she had finished off with a deft knot.

She resumed her seat, her thoughts in turmoil. What the dickens was going on? Wicken would not lend himself to an abduction. He would—

Looking straight ahead, she asked, "Why is Wicken driving?"

"I begged him to. My coachman is too old for the long drive into Hertfordshire, and I sent my groom ahead to warn my grandfather."

Slowly she turned. "You're taking me to Stanford Hall? Why?"

"To marry you."

Her heart leaped into her throat. She searched his face, but his features were carefully controlled and gave no clue of his thoughts. Only in the narrow slits of eye showing beneath his lashes she saw an expression such as she had never seen before.

Anger, resentment, suspicion melted under that look. Clutching the edge of the seat so she wouldn't throw her arms around him, she said, "So that's what Wicken meant. He's a bit premature, though, since you may not be a duke for a long time."

He was watching her from beneath lazily drooping lids. "You won't mind being a marchioness, will you?"

Mind! Her blood raced so fast that it burned her skin. She wouldn't mind being a beggar's wife, if he were the beggar. But if this was a proposal of marriage, why wasn't he hugging and kissing her, telling her he loved her?

"Why, Dev? Why do you want to marry me?"

"Because I love you."

The words she had longed to hear. But instead of sending her into raptures, they made her want to cry. Devil a bit! She never cried. And she wouldn't give up on him either. She wanted to marry him, but not while he was behaving like a dull stick. He was Devil Mackenzie, a rake, an experienced lover of many women. And that was whom she wanted. She wouldn't settle for less.

"I shan't marry you," she said gruffly.

"What?" Dev shot up, wincing as he hit his head on the carriage roof and jarred his arm.

Slowly, he sat down again, and Nell knew the satisfaction of having pierced his calm. No longer was his face expressionless. He looked incredulous, confused, and not a little put out.

She relaxed against the squabs, folded her hands in her lap, and once again stared straight ahead. "Just because you mouthed three words, you cannot expect me to be swept off my feet."

"Oh, I see," he muttered, rubbing the top of his head. "You want me to kneel and all that. But, dash it, Nell! I was down on my knees twice this night, and both times you rebuffed me."

"Dev, I'm disappointed in you. I don't want a formal proposal. Your reputation is such that I expect something a little more fiery, more persuasive."

She felt him stir beside her and risked a sidelong peek. He was studying her intently, the beginning of his devilish smile shaping on his mouth.

Satisfied, she shifted her gaze to her hands. "But, perhaps, you are of the old school? Perhaps you believe that ardor and passion are for a man's mistress only, while his intended must make do with dutiful affection?''

"Nell, you wretch! How can you sit there looking demure as a nun's hen, all the while enticing me to passion? I thought I'd scare you if I were to declare my love the way I want.''

His attack—and there was no other word to describe his sudden lunge, the tightening of his arms around her as he drew her onto his knees—contained all the passion and ardor Nell could possibly want.

"Your arm," she murmured in a halfhearted attempt to bring him to his senses, then forgot all about it when his mouth claimed hers in a ruthless and most satisfying kiss.

"Now, will you marry me?" His hands played in her hair, ran delicious patterns up and down her arms and her back. Through his shirt and the thin cotton of her nightgown, she felt his heart beat against her breast.

With a squeak of dismay, she pushed away from him. "Dev, how could you? You carried me off in my night rail. No clergyman in his right mind will marry us.''

He grinned. "That's exactly the argument I used with Bess. Or, rather, Wicken did after I convinced him of my honorable intentions toward you."

Indignation threatened to flare again. "They all knew?''

Catching her in his good arm, he dropped a kiss onto the tip of her nose, effectively squashing all but the wish to be kissed and held forever.

"They know that I am determined to marry you, and that you, my love, can be as stubborn as a mule when you get some maggoty notion in your pretty head—like my wanting to marry you for the house. In any case, there is a cloak bag in the boot with a gown and some few necessities. And tomorrow Bess will follow with your trunks."

She had ceased to listen after he mentioned the house. "Dev? About the house." Her fingers toyed with the collar of his shirt, which had started to droop since the removal of his cravat. "When I put away the cards, I couldn't help but notice your discard pile."

"What about it, my love?" Distracted by the play of her fingers against his neck, he did not pay attention to the tingle at the base of his skull until it was almost too late.

"Did you let me win?"

"Dash it, Nell. Why would I do a daft thing like that?"

How strange it was, she mused, spellbound by his guileless blue eyes, that she was most strongly reminded of Lucifer when he looked most innocent.

"My turn to question, madam. What kind of arrangement," he asked with a hint of sternness, "do you have with Sir Nathan?"

"Lud! I forgot." She yanked at the curtain on the carriage window. Pale dawn and a rosy hint of sunrise greeted her. She let the curtain drop. With a stricken look in her eyes, she turned to Dev. "We must turn back. Something I must do, but I cannot tell you about it. Please, Dev. Will you turn back?"

"No." Firmly he pulled her back into his arms. "If it has to do with the thirty thousand pounds you offered for my house, you can forget about it. Sir Nathan will have a note with his morning chocolate, informing him of our upcoming marriage. Any business he may have with you, he can discuss with both of us after our honeymoon."

"You know about Sir Nathan? And you won't mind my working—"

She was ruthlessly silenced by his kiss. The motion of the carriage, his arms cradling her, and the mind-robbing sensations evoked by his mouth and tongue, were enough to distract a female of even greater willfulness than Nell. At present, she admitted, she had no will of her own.

Naturally, this state of affairs could not last forever. Dev was not surprised when Nell began to squirm and finally nipped his lower lip with sharp little teeth.

"Brat!" He gently shook her by the shoulders. "My pesky little brat. Just wait until we're married."

She regarded him wistfully. "Is a pesky little brat better than a pocket Venus?"

"For me, a thousand times better."

Again he claimed her mouth, but Nell had just remembered what she meant to ask him. Resolutely she pushed against his chest until he released her sufficiently for speech.

"What do you think your grandfather will say when we arrive on his doorstep?"

"He'll greet you with open arms." Dev smiled the wicked smile that had captured her heart over two years ago. "I've already told him that I'm marrying you for the sake of Fane House."

Warner Regency Romances

☐ CHARLESTON TANGLE
Joan E. Overfield
(D35-156, $3.50, U.S.A.) (D35-157, $4.50, Canada)
Set in Charleston, South Carolina, a charming story about a young widow who falls in love with a dashing English gentleman.

☐ THE DANDY'S DECEPTION
Philippa Castle
(D35-008, $3.50, U.S.A.) (D35-009, $4.50, Canada)
A delightful romance in which a blue-eyed beauty and a handsome Earl find rapturous love, in spite of their families' interferences.

 **Warner Books P.O. Box 690
New York, NY 10019**

Please send me the books I have checked. I enclose a check or money order (not cash), plus 95¢ per order and 95¢ per copy to cover postage and handling.* (Allow 4-6 weeks for delivery.)

___Please send me your free mail order catalog. (If ordering only the catalog, include a large self-addressed, stamped envelope.)

Name _____

Address _____

City _____ State _____ Zip _____

*New York and California residents add applicable sales tax.   386